ESPECIALLY FOR GIRLS™
presents

Valerie

Original Title: Sneaking Around

by Barbara Steiner

With a closing statement by Dr. Steve Bank

FIELD PUBLICATIONS
Middletown, Connecticut

For my friend Beverly Day

This book is a presentation of **Especially for Girls**™,
Weekly Reader Books. Weekly Reader Books offers
book clubs for children from preschool through high school.
For further information write to: **Weekly Reader Books,**
4343 Equity Drive, Columbus, Ohio 43228.

Cover art created by Hal Frenck.
Cover art © 1987 by Field Publications.

Chapter 1

"You have to help me!" Valerie Harding paced the floor in front of a table at The Speak. She tossed her long brown hair about like a thoroughbred horse would toss her mane. Then she flopped in a chair. "The dance is Wednesday night. It's formal, and I don't even own a formal. Dori?" Valerie appealed to Dori Fiedler, who was a terrific seamstress.

"I don't know, Valerie," Dori said. "Sure, I could make you a simple formal. And that would be your style, something simple and dramatic, but . . ."

"We don't like the sneaking around, Valerie," Sunny Kiefer finished Dori's sentence. "Even if it is your mother and not ours."

"You guys have been talking behind my back, haven't you?" Valerie accused. "You've already planned not to help me go out with Carl."

Sunny looked at Dori and Kristen. Kristen Mc-Dowell shrugged and faced Valerie. "We *have* talked about it, Valerie. Did you think we wouldn't? This is the most exciting thing happening right now. How could we *not* talk about it?"

"We don't want you to think we're ganging up on you, Valerie," Dori said, "but . . ."

"You are. I knew you would." Valerie jumped up and flew over to the counter to refill her soda. It wasn't doing a bit of good to get angry with her friends, but she couldn't help it. She felt frustrated and angry and at a loss for what to do.

Her problem had started at the fall fundraiser, the carnival that Columbine Middle School had held in November. Carl Bentson, a high school boy who performed magic shows as "Carl the Magnificent" had been invited to do a magic act as part of the program. Seized by one of her many bold ideas, Valerie had called him and volunteered to be his assistant. The whole idea had worked out better than she expected, and she had fallen head over heels for Carl. Apparently the feeling was mutual. Carl had asked her to the high school Christmas dance. The dance wasn't the problem, though. It was her mother, who had laid down a hard-and-fast rule that Valerie couldn't date until she was sixteen.

Valerie tapped her glass on the counter, impatient with the girl serving drinks. Lifting the glass, she filled her mouth with ice and crunched it. She knew what she had to do. She'd appeal to her friends' sense of fairness. Her mother's rules were not fair.

She approached their table again. "Look, guys. You know my mother isn't being fair. You're the only friends I have. If you won't help me, who will? Didn't we take a sacred vow to stick together? Through thick or thin?"

"This is too thick for us," Kristen joked, flashing her big smile. But Valerie didn't smile back. How could anyone kid around about the most important thing that had happened to her in her whole life? A high school guy, a genuine older man, had asked her out. She absolutely refused to call him and say she couldn't go. Especially now that she'd told him she'd love to be his date for the dance.

School had let out on Friday for the holiday break, and the four friends had gathered on Saturday at The Speak Easy, their usual hangout, for lunch before they went shopping together. Sunny had gone to the dance at Columbine the night before with Peter Mandala, her steady boyfriend. Dori showed up with Roger Rainey, which was a surprise to everyone except her three friends. They knew that Dori and Roger had been seeing each other since the carnival, but disguised as two clowns named Bashful and Funky. The two clowns finally revealed their identities and came to the dance dressed as themselves. Valerie was glad that Dori and Roger had finally gotten together, but now it was her turn to start dating a guy she liked. And she was crazy about Carl.

"Why didn't you ask Carl to meet you at the dance on Friday night, Valerie?" Sunny asked. "That would have been safe."

"I did. He had a magic show to do."

"Then why didn't he ask you to be his assistant for the show?" Dori wanted to know. She had made Valerie a beautiful sparkly blue jacket with velveteen lapels for the carnival.

"He said he'd work me into the act gradually," Valerie answered. "He does want me to keep helping him, but there wasn't time to practice."

"How are you going to get out of the house to do shows?" Sunny asked. "Look, why don't you just talk to your mother, Valerie? Tell her about Carl. Bring Carl over and introduce him. She can see he's a perfectly normal human being, not some weirdo or junkie."

"She wouldn't care if he were Mr. Nice Guy U.S.A.," Valerie moaned. "You know I can't talk to my mother like you can to yours, Sunny. My mother is totally narrow-minded when it comes to my dating anyone, especially a guy older than I am, someone in high school. With a car." Valerie pushed her mother out of her mind and let thoughts of Carl take over.

"I think she's in love with his car, not him," Kristen observed. "Don't you guys agree?" Sometimes Kristen's big smile was too much for Valerie to tolerate. Even now Kristen was laughing and kidding when she was the only one of the foursome left without a guy. Valerie would have died if she were in Kristen's shoes.

Sunny and Dori joined in Kristen's laughter. Finally Valerie had to smile despite her dilemma.

"Come on, guys. You know I wouldn't be so dumb." Valerie tried again to persuade them to help her get out of her house safely. "Look, we need a plan. Dori makes me a dress. It won't be the first time she's sewed for me. There's nothing wrong with that. Agreed?"

"OK, we're not against a new dress, Valerie." Sunny looked at Dori as if to say, "What can we say?" Valerie knew she was winning.

"Then I tell Mom I'll be spending the night at

Dori's. It'll be two days before Christmas. I'll tell Mom we're wrapping packages and making candy."

"Worst case scenario," Kristen said, wrapping a finger around one of her blonde curls. "Your mom calls about nine o'clock and wants to talk to you."

"Why would she do that?" Valerie polished off her hamburger and spoke with her mouth partly full. "She never wants to talk to me at home. Why would she want to talk to me at Dori's?" She licked the catsup from her fingers and wiped her hands on her napkin.

"I think you're misjudging your mother," Sunny said, pushing her hair away from her face. "We won't lie if she does call."

"Fine. If she does, I'll take the consequences." Valerie leaned back and fluffed out her hair over her jean jacket. The four girls put on their coats in preparation for leaving The Speak. "But you know how Mom is. She has to know where I am every minute. Who I'm with. How long I'll be gone. You all aren't there every night at dinnertime when I get the third degree on what my day was like, what I did after school."

Valerie's mom was secretary to a lawyer in west Denver, so she never got home until almost six on weekdays, and sometimes she had to go to work on Saturday. Her mom's getting a job had been the best thing that ever happened to Valerie. At least her mother wasn't there, demanding that Valerie be home from school by three-thirty.

For some people, losing a father would be the worst thing that could possibly happen to them. But Valerie hardly remembered her father. He was some vague shadow in her childhood, her only memory was how tall he was. Of course, she was so little, any father would seem tall. For a while after her parents' divorce, there were presents on birthdays and Christmas, but in recent years her father had sent only a card with some money. Her mother still received child support payments, and Valerie guessed that was where her generous allowance came from since there wasn't a lot of extra money around her house. Because Valerie spent most of her allowance on her karate lessons, she never had much left for clothes, makeup, and record albums. Out of necessity, Valerie had adopted a unique and flamboyant style of dress, put together with thrift shop finds and other items most girls her age wouldn't think of.

The foursome grabbed a bus for the mall and stopped talking about Valerie's problem with her mother. With Christmas fast approaching, they talked of their gift lists and making their money stretch to cover all their shopping.

"What are you getting Peter?" Kristen asked Sunny. Sunny had been dating Peter, her super cute basketball player, since early in the school year.

"I finally got this great idea," Sunny answered. "You guys have to help me find a stuffed gorilla." Peter had worn a gorilla suit at the carnival, and Sunny had dressed as a gorilla trainer.

"Perfect!" Dori squealed at the idea. "I'm getting Roger something for his clowning. I wish I could find one of those stiff leashes attached to a dog harness. One of the students at the high school had one, but when I asked where he got it, he said Disney World."

"You could jump on a plane and go get one," Kristen suggested. "Take me with you, though. It'll be consolation for not having a guy to shop for. Otherwise, I may have to console myself with a box of chocolate-covered cherries.''

"Then you'll ruin your figure for good, and it'll be even harder to get a boyfriend,'' Valerie teased.

"What figure?'' Kristen looked down at her "pleasingly plump'' body. "I've been watching my weight all fall, and nothing has happened.''

"Bad joke. I didn't mean it *that* way, Dodo,'' Valerie commented again. She spent a lot of time either teasing Kristen or frankly criticizing her eating habits.

"You guys.'' Sunny laughed. "If I didn't know you were best friends, I'd worry about you.''

"It's a love-hate relationship.'' Kristen punched Valerie, who struck a karate pose in response.

"Look at this place!'' Dori exclaimed as they enter the huge mall. "There's hardly room to walk. We should plan where we'll meet if we get separated.''

"We could rope up together, like mountain climbers.'' Sunny took Dori's arm. "Why didn't we shop early?''

"We did,'' Kristen reminded her. "But Santa wasn't here.''

"You going to ask him to bring you some glasses so you can see the truth at last?'' Valerie asked.

"Never. Do you think there's such a thing as low-calorie chocolate-covered cherries?'' Kristen made her face especially sad.

"No such luck.'' Valerie laughed and puffed out her cheeks as if to show how she'd look if *she* were in love with chocolate the way Kristen was. "Hey, here's Cloth World. Let's go there first and find me some fabric for a formal.''

"You won't give up this idea, Valerie?" Sunny half pleaded.

"Absolutely not," Valerie said. "If you guys won't help me, I'll find another way to pull it off. I'm going to the Christmas dance at the high school with Carl even if my mom finds out and kills me later. At least I'll die happy."

Her mother *would* kill her if she found out. Or ground her forever. But Valerie was sure it was worth the risk. She'd never met a guy like Carl Bentson in her life, and she might never meet anyone like him again. Carl the Magnificent. He sure was, and he was crazy about her too. No way was she going to give him up.

Chapter 2

By Monday Valerie was so excited she could hardly stand it. She'd better cool it, though, or her mother would ask what was going on. Valerie's mother was perceptive as well as suspicious.

"What are you doing today, Valerie?"

It was a holiday. Why hadn't Valerie had the good sense to lie in bed till her mother left for work? But she was too wired to stay in bed. Besides, she'd told Mr. Warrington she'd help him with the beginner adult karate classes at noon. She was learning to teach and he gave her a discount on her class fees when she helped. Maybe by the time she was sixteen or seventeen she could get a real job at the studio.

"I'm helping with classes at the studio," Valerie said, spreading blueberry jam on her toast. The smell was delicious. She shoveled in her eggs hungrily. She was always starved in the morning—another reason she'd gotten up. Valerie could fix her own breakfast, but sometimes, if she wasn't running late, her mother would make omelets. Usually Valerie enjoyed those breakfasts—but not today. Today, of all days, her mother had time to have a second cup of coffee and question Valerie.

Valerie thought her mother was a beautiful woman, although the two of them had totally different styles. Where Valerie liked to dress dramatically, her mother was conservative. This morning she had her long black hair pulled into a bun at the nape of her neck. Only a sheer white blouse with a ruffled jabot kept her mother's gray pinstripe suit from looking masculine. Valerie decided her mother had virtually memorized all the current books for women on how to dress for success. And she obviously was following the books' suggestions to the letter. On her feet were plain black pumps with two-inch heels, even though Valerie's mother, like Valerie, was tall. Height was practically the only trait that Valerie and her mother had in common.

Valerie wondered if she got her richly colored red-brown hair from her father, but she never dared ask. Any mention of Valerie's father put her mother in a bad mood for days. You'd think that after ten years her mother would have forgiven him for whatever it was that caused the divorce.

"I don't like your hanging out at that place, Valerie. You know I don't. It's bad enough that you take those lessons."

"Helping teach classes isn't hanging out, Mom. You make it sound like the neighborhood bar."

"This neighborhood has no bars, Valerie. That's why I keep struggling to make these awful house payments. Maybe I should give up and get us a nice condo, but I hate the thought of moving. I know this neighborhood is safe, and you do have nice friends here."

At least her mother liked her friends. Valerie's life would be worse if her mom disapproved of Sunny, Kristen, and Dori. She couldn't imagine moving and having to make new friends. The thought made her shiver.

"You're not dressed warmly enough for going out, Valerie. Why you won't wear that nice down jacket I bought you is beyond me. You insist on that denim jacket in the middle of winter." Sometimes it seemed to Valerie all her mom could do was preach.

"Mom, everyone at school wears denim jackets all year round," Valerie responded in a careful tone, trying to pacify her.

"Do they all have silver studs on them like some motorcycle maniac? All those patches sewn on the back and those buttons on the front? What *do* all those *say* anyway?" Her mother leaned forward to see Valerie's button collection. Valerie got up and went to the fridge to get another glass of milk.

Valerie kept her back turned and tried to keep her mouth shut. Nothing she wore pleased her mother. She knew that. It was easier to avoid a confrontation, so she did. Eventually she knew her mom would stop her harangue of Valerie's taste in clothes. One topic she never let up on was the karate, however.

"I'll never understand why you gave up your ballet for that—that macho self-defense stuff. You always looked so lovely in your ballet costumes. And you *were* good, Valerie. You were good enough to have made a career of dance."

"Karate isn't just self-defense, Mother. That's only a small part of it. Karate is a sport and an art form." There she went again, getting sucked into arguing with her mother.

Valerie had taken ballet for as long as she could remember. And she had been good at it. But suddenly it had seemed so . . . so . . . *lady-like* wasn't the word she searched for. Boring maybe. And prissy . . . that was it—prissy. All the sweet little girls and the sweet, dreamy music. Floating around, little swans or butterflies in tulle skirts.

Karate was much better suited to Valerie's temperament. Not that she was violent, or even super aggressive. But it was more like a sport, and she loved the challenge. Her training in dance had helped her pick it up quickly. Karate was a sport that took grace, precision, and the strength that years of ballet had given her.

Admit it, Valerie, a little voice prodded her. You liked karate much more once you found that your mother hated it—the idea, everything about it. A little smile escaped, and Valerie hid it behind her glass of milk. Something in her made her keep annoying her mother any way she could. It was so easy to do.

It seemed a good way to get back at her mother for demanding that Valerie follow so many rules, for interfering so much in Valerie's life. Valerie figured her mother would oppose any decision she made. That was the main reason she wasn't going to tell her mother about Carl. If the president of the United States had a son Valerie's age, and if he wanted to take Valerie out, her mom would say no so fast even the president would be surprised.

Her mother told Valerie a long time ago that she was not to date until she was sixteen, and then only when her mother met the guy and decided he was "nice." Valerie assumed "nice" meant good enough. Or a safe person to trust Valerie with. Would any guy ever be good enough for her to go with? Why couldn't her mother trust her? Didn't her mother think she had good judgment? Why couldn't she trust Valerie to choose a guy for herself?

"You're going to be late, Mom," Valerie reminded her mother, who had finished her coffee and was now up, clearing the table. She didn't want to listen to the anti-karate lecture again. She'd heard it dozens of times. "Thanks for making the omelet. I'll clean up the dishes."

"Thanks, Valerie. Be careful going to that place. And I'll expect you to be here this afternoon if I call."

"I was going over to Dori's after lunch."

"Well, OK. But don't stay all afternoon. Her mother won't want you hanging around there all the time."

Valerie didn't dare say that Dori's parents were never at home. That would be something else for her mother to worry about. Or a reason to forbid Valerie to go there.

Rinsing the dishes and putting them in the dishwasher took Valerie only a few minutes. She wiped the counter tops, the table, and quickly straightened up around the kitchen. Then she put her karate things into her canvas shoulder bag and hurried out the door to catch the bus to the studio.

"Hi, Valerie," Mr. Warrington greeted her as she breezed into the studio. Her mood always improved after she left home. It was like escaping from a prison where she had to live part time.

"Hi, Al. What time does the beginner adult class start? I want to work out first."

"No problem. There's a beginner class at ten and another at eleven. Then open workouts at noon. Come help with as many classes as you can. I'm glad to have you here. With kids off for the holiday, we'll get bigger crowds during the day. We may have more mothers at noon too." He laughed.

Valerie tried to envision her mother studying karate, but it was impossible. She glanced at her brightly colored watch and was pleased to discover she had nearly an hour for herself.

Finding an empty room, she changed quickly into the traditional white *gi,* the loose-fitting pants and wraparound top she wore for practice and lessons. She had reached the top brown belt, and was working toward a first-degree black belt. Al Warrington was amazed at how fast Valerie progressed in the sport. She had even skipped one of the lower belts. But she worked very hard, loving everything about karate. Except for her relationship with her mother—and she might never win where her mother was concerned—Valerie felt she had much more control of herself and her life since she'd started karate. She felt stronger mentally as well as physically.

Assuming the beginning pose, Valerie practiced the formal movements and quick thrusts of her feet and hands. She sparred with an imaginary opponent. The exercises, called *kata,* concentrated on form, speed, and power. She found it not unlike ballet, which was much more formal than other styles of dance.

After about half an hour, Valerie stopped to take out the short *sai* sword she had checked out at the desk. Only since beginning the black belt classes had she earned the right to work with Japanese weapons. The three-pronged knife, although missing its sharp blades, still frightened her a little. She treated it with respect, practicing the quick thrusts with it in her hand.

Wouldn't her mother die to see her handling the weapon with such skill? She laughed, but felt a touch of sadness. Her mother had refused to come to any of the demonstrations or competitions after refusing to pay for the lessons in the first place. By contrast, her mom had always been in the front row at her ballet recitals. She had taken pride in Valerie's ballet gear, sparing no expense on shoes, leotards, and performance costumes.

Sometimes Valerie worked to help pay for her karate classes or equipment, cleaning up the studio or doing odd jobs for Al. She'd told him her problem, without going into detail, about her mother's hatred for the sport; and Al seemed to understand. If she could only speed up her life and become old enough to teach, it would help. But no one would take a class, or let their children take a class, from a fourteen-year-old girl. They'd think she could babysit, but not teach karate.

The morning flew by. Valerie had a great sense of well-being when she was at the studio—learning, practicing, or teaching. She would have loved to stay all day, but she needed to go to Dori's and try on her dress.

Hunger and the thought of her up coming date

eventually tugged Valerie back into real life. She hadn't thought of Carl the whole morning. That seemed impossible, but now she tuned into the tremor in her stomach that had nothing to do with hunger.

She hadn't told Carl she was fast becoming a karate master. Would that scare him? Put him off? Lots of the guys teased her about it. There was so much she didn't know about Carl Bentson, and he knew very little about her. She could hardly wait to spend more time with him and get better acquainted. Would he like her once he knew her better? She couldn't wait for Wednesday night and the dance, a high school dance. This was going to be the best—and the scariest, she had to admit—holiday ever.

Chapter 3

Valerie bounced up to Dori's front door and pushed the bell. "Hello, Wong Ti," she called. It was unbelievable weather for late December, and the Fiedlers' gardener was mixing fertilizer into the flower beds around the Fiedlers' huge house. Valerie had always thought the English Tudor-style house looked like a storybook castle. But Dori made a very shy princess. Valerie whirled around on the sidewalk while she waited for Dori to answer the door.

"Valerie," Dori called. "What are you doing?"

"Whirling." Valerie laughed. "We should be outside, Dori. You'd think it was spring."

"You have more energy than anyone I know, Valerie." Dori closed the door behind them as Valerie skipped into the house. "Sometimes I'm envious. I'd get twice as much done."

"Now that we know about your secret life as a clown, Dori, I'd say you get a lot more done than anyone ever dreamed you did. To think we were convinced you were studying all that time."

Both girls laughed. Dori had finally let her friends know she was Bashful, the sad clown. She'd kept it secret for many months, letting her secret out only because of the school carnival. And because of Roger Rainey.

"What are you and Roger doing for Christmas, Dori? You looked great together at the dance Friday."

"Thanks, Valerie. Want something to eat? Yes, of course, you do. Why do I ask?" Everyone knew about Valerie's appetite. And even though she'd eaten the lunch she'd taken to the studio, she was starving again. "We'll get together Christmas Eve. Roger is taking me someplace wonderful for dinner. He won't say where."

Valerie peered over Dori's shoulder into the fridge in the big kitchen. "Have any ice cream?"

"No wonder Kristen has a love-hate relationship with you, Valerie. You can eat anything and tons of it without putting on a pound." Dori reached into the freezer for a pint of gourmet ice cream, vanilla red raspberry swirl. She divided the contents into two bowls and they took it upstairs to polish off while they worked.

"Poor Kristen." Valerie licked her spoon after every bite. "Everything she eats settles around her middle. I wonder if her mother was heavy."

"It must be awful not to know who your real parents are," Dori said, curling up on her bed until she finished her snack. "I think you'd always wonder."

"But she has such a great family." Valerie was often envious of Kristen's closeness with her parents and sisters.

Dori read her mind as she often did with her friends.

"We're lucky, Valerie, to have such good friends. We're like four sisters."

"Yeah." Valerie was careful not to dwell too long on the idea of families. "But where's my dress? I figured you'd be half finished."

"Don't panic. I'll get it done. But I had a great idea, using this pattern we picked out, but improving on it." Dori set her dish on the bedside table and hurried over to her sewing table. "Look, do you like Grecian? It'll make you look older." She showed Valerie the sketch she had made of a gown.

"Wow! You're going to make me *that*? Do I *like* it? I'd have to be *crazy* not to." Valerie danced around, holding the sketch. It was a very plain design, but one shoulder was bare and from the other the fabric draped and flowed gracefully all the way to the floor.

"If he brings you flowers, you'll have to pin them to your waist. Too bad you can't tell him to bring you a wrist corsage."

"I don't care if he brings flowers or not. Oh, Dori, you're a genius." Valerie threw her arms around Dori and gave her a bear hug. "I'm so lucky to have a future high-fashion dress designer for a friend."

"It's fun sewing for you, Valerie. You're great when it comes to clothes. I'd never dare wear something like this."

"But you're so cute now, Dori, since you had your hair cut and permed and got contacts."

"If you asked me to choose between being cute and being glamorous, Valerie, there would be no choice. *You* are glamorous."

Glamorous? Valerie liked the sound of it. Could Carl handle her being glamorous? It was terribly hard to stand still while Dori cut, pinned, and draped material.

"Be still, Valerie," Dori said, pinning the fabric. "How do you expect me to work without sticking you?"

"I can't be still, Dori. Go ahead and stick me or pinch me, so I can be sure I'm not dreaming. I'm going to a Christmas dance at the high school with a high school guy. Eeeek!" Valerie squealed to let out some of the pent-up excitement that kept her from holding still.

Dori stopped pinning. "I hope you're going out with him because you like him, Valerie. Not because he's older."

"Of course, I like him, silly. I'm not going out with him *just* because he's older."

"Maybe you need an older guy, Valerie. You and Sunny seem so much older than Kristen and I. And goodness knows you *look* older. You have a great figure. I'm going to be flat forever."

Valerie giggled. "Thanks, Dori. It's probably all the exercise I get that helps me stay in shape."

They talked, and Dori sewed and fitted until she had the dress at a stage where she could finish it without Valerie.

"Here's half of what I owe you for the sewing, Dori." Valerie handed Dori a stack of dollar bills she'd saved. "Can I pay you the rest next week, or do you need it for Christmas?"

"I don't need it at all, Valerie. Pay me when you can, or let me give you the sewing job for Christmas," Dori offered.

"You're too generous, Dori. Not a good business

practice. No, I'll pay you next week. I usually get a check from my father for Christmas." Valerie took the dress off slowly. She didn't want to think about her father because she didn't know what to think. He was like a shadow in her past. A real Santa who sent money occasionally.

"OK, see you Wednesday, Valerie. About four, so I can have time to make any last-minute adjustments while you guys fix dinner."

"Sure. I'll be too nervous to eat but I want plenty of time to get ready."

"I'm still not convinced that what we're doing is right, Valerie," Dori said, walking Valerie downstairs and to the door.

"It'll be OK, Dori. Believe me." Valerie reassured her.

Slowly, Valerie walked home. She didn't like having to deceive her mother any more than her friends liked it, but it was the only way she could go to the dance with Carl. She wished her mother was more reasonable; but since she wasn't, Valerie had no choice.

Well, she could have told Carl no, but that wasn't a choice she liked.

Wednesday afternoon dragged by like Christmas Eve used to when Valerie was little. Now Christmas for her was something to get through. But her date with Carl made her usual holiday blues disappear. She'd talked to him twice, and he seemed to be looking forward to it, too. Wait till he saw her dress!

Tucking the sparkly blue shoes she'd worn in the carnival magic show into the bottom of her overnight bag, Valerie tried to make sure she had everything she needed to get ready. She had a white shawl bought in Mexico on one of her Mom's rare vacations. It was bulky, and Valerie wished she'd taken it over to Dori's on Monday.

Her mother had nearly upset Valerie's plans by protesting her spending the night with Dori. "I'm taking Thursday off, Valerie. It'll make a four-day holiday. We could go someplace together. Colorado Springs, maybe, or Glenwood Springs. We could swim in the hot pool."

Valerie knew her mother didn't much enjoy the Christmas holidays either, but four days alone with her mother? No way.

"Oh, I can't, Mom. We've had this planned forever. We're going to wrap presents and make candy, Christmas cookies. Sunny and Dori are giving their boyfriends a care package as well as a present."

Valerie wanted her mother to hear that two of her friends had steady boyfriends. Maybe her mom would soften about the age-sixteen dating rule.

"That's nice," said her mother as if she hardly heard what Valerie had said. "Well, maybe Ruth Berger would like to go to a movie."

"That's a good idea, Mom. There are lots of good movies playing around."

Throughout the day all Valerie could think of was getting out of the house before her mother, for some reason or other, came home early and stopped Valerie from leaving. She fought down this terrible feeling that something could still go wrong.

Arriving breathless at Dori's, Valerie balanced on her skateboard outside the front door. Dori poked her cute pixie face out. "Good, I have only the hem left to do after you try it on in your heels."

They rushed upstairs. Dori slipped the dress over Valerie's head. "No peeking." She stepped back to look at her creation.

"How can I wait?" Valerie wanted to run to the mirror. The soft material felt delicious against her skin and the chiffon drape tickled her arm as she moved. The color was rich cream.

"We'll have a showing for Kristen and Sunny. Stand *still.* I need to measure the hem in only one place. Then I'll put it on the ironing board to pin it."

The doorbell rang as Valerie slid out of the dress and pulled on her pink sweats. "I'll get it. You sew."

Dori laughed and agreed. "Help yourself in the kitchen," she called as Valerie ran downstairs.

"Oh, aren't you dying of excitement?" Kristen said, as she came in, Sunny right behind her.

"I am. I am." Valerie wiggled and jumped as if to show them how excited she was. "Dori said we should go ahead and start dinner since she's still sewing. I know I won't be able to eat a bite."

"That'll be the day, Scarlett," Sunny teased. "You'll pig out now so you can pretend to have no appetite later."

"I *am* hungry," Valerie admitted. But how could she be? Her stomach felt as if someone were inside doing back flips.

The girls knew Dori's kitchen well, since it was there they usually gathered to cook or when they were on a sleepover. Dori's parents were research scientists, psychologists actually, at the university and quite often they had lab experiments going on that they couldn't leave. The foursome liked the chance to be alone and gossip.

Soon the kitchen smelled of spaghetti sauce. It was the kind you get from a jar, rather than cook all day, but it was filling and easy to prepare. Sunny shredded lettuce for a salad. Kristen sliced French bread and spread butter on each slice.

"I suppose Valerie won't want any garlic on hers," Kristen said. "Good thing I don't have a date. I want tons." She shook garlic powder over half the bread, leaving some plain.

"Don't you sabotage my evening!" Valerie dashed over to make sure of Kristen's actions.

"Do you think Carl will make her disappear if she has bad breath?" Sunny asked with a serious tone of voice. "Then he'll be free to look over the stag line."

Dori came into the kitchen in time to hear the remark. "Wait till you see her. He'll have to make the stag line disappear. Or sprinkle magic dust over her to get one dance."

"Where's my dress?" Valerie asked.

"Safe in the closet. You don't want spaghetti sauce on it, do you? *I* don't, after all my work."

"Oh, thanks, Dori. You're the greatest." Valerie loaded her plate. Then about halfway through the meal, with everyone chattering, mostly teasing her, she lost her appetite.

"Uh-oh, this is serious," Kristen said. "The day that Valerie stops eating, we know she's bad off. I'll finish yours." Kristen reached for Valerie's plate.

Valerie had even lost the desire to tease Kristen about eating everything in sight—even someone else's leftovers. "I think I'm going to be sick," she announced with certainty.

Her three friends screamed and laughed. "Take deep breaths," advised Sunny. "Want to lie down?" asked Dori. But Kristen ran to the fridge and poured Valerie some lemon-lime soda. "Here, you'll recover."

Valerie rolled her eyes at Kristen, who grinned her big grin. She sipped the bubbly drink while everyone scarfed down their food and reached for more.

"Sunny, you and Kristen do dishes while I help Valerie dress," suggested Dori. "She needs to get ready—if she can stand up."

"I'm fine now," Valerie said, and she was. She raced upstairs ahead of Dori.

In no time Valerie stood in front of Dori's full-length mirror. "Is that me?" she asked, amazed at her appearance. The slightest touch of makeup complemented her brown eyes and naturally rosy cheeks. The fabric of the dress had a soft luster that shimmered in the light. She had washed her hair in the morning, brushing it when it was dry until it glowed with its coppery streaks. Now it floated around her shoulders, tickling her one bare shoulder.

"Come on up!" Dori shouted to the crew in the kitchen. "Cinderella is ready for the ball."

They clattered upstairs.

"Wow!" said Kristen. "You look beautiful, Valerie."

"Do we know you?" Sunny laughed softly. "Carl won't be able to dance."

"Or pull any rabbits from his hat." Dori giggled. "You'd better be careful, Valerie. Magicians have quick hands."

"If he doesn't behave, I'll give him a karate chop,"

said Valerie, twirling again.

"It's Valerie," said Kristen. "We do know her and she hasn't really changed."

The doorbell bonged from the hall.

"There he is," said Dori. "Ready, Valerie?"

Valerie took a deep breath. "I don't think so," she whispered. "I'm not sure I can handle this."

"Look," Sunny said in a no-nonsense tone. "We're risking our necks for you, Valerie. You're going if we have to carry you down there."

With a friend supporting her on either side, Valerie floated down the stairway. On the outside she was as calm and cool as a fashion model. But inside she wanted to turn cartwheels. This was real. She was a Cinderella. Was Carl really her prince?

Chapter 4

Carl's approval shone on his face. "Wow, Valerie, you look fantastic."

Three sets of giggles came from behind Valerie.

"Thank you, Carl," Valerie said. "Do you know my friends? This is Dori Fiedler. She made my dress. Sunny Kiefer, Kristen McDowell," Valerie introduced. "We're spending the night at Dori's."

"You don't live here?" Carl asked.

"No, Dori lives here. Ready to go?" Valerie was ready to be alone with Carl. And although he *seemed* at ease having four girls at the door when it opened, she couldn't be sure he really was all that comfortable. Magicians had to be good actors.

Carl helped Valerie into the car, then went around to the driver's side. He was dressed in a dark blue suit with a vest that had a shiny front, satin or taffeta, Valerie guessed. He probably wore it in his shows. A dark red tie and his white shirt complemented the vest nicely.

Before starting the car, Carl handed Valerie a corsage box. "I forgot to ask what color your dress was, Valerie. And I got one of those styles that you can wear on your arm. I hope that's OK."

Yellow roses. Valerie loved yellow roses. "It's perfect, Carl. You're not just a magician, you're a mind reader."

He was smooth, really smooth. Valerie knew he must have a lot of experience with dating. He didn't seem nervous at all. She pushed down her fears, trying to act natural with him.

He drove an older model sports car, the kind with flames painted on the hood. At least his driving didn't match the racy style of the bright red car.

Valerie studied Carl's profile while he concentrated on driving the short distance to the school. His nose was straight and fit his perfectly shaped features. Valerie wondered if he was part Greek or Italian. His hair was a black so dark it looked blue in certain lights, and it had a slight curl to it. Wasn't she lucky that a guy like this was crazy about her?

"Who said he was crazy about you?" a little voice said. "Well," she answered it, "this is an important dance, and he *is* taking me."

They pulled into the parking lot at the school. Valerie was glad it wasn't snowing. She wouldn't have wanted to get off at the door without him or get her satiny shoes wet. She stayed in the car until he came around to open the door and help her out. His touch sent little shivers all over her. It had grown cooler out, almost cold, but the December night sparkled with a million stars. Valerie felt like one of them. She pulled her shawl closer as they hurried into the building.

Music spilled out into the halls as they headed for the gymnasium. Carl handed his tickets to a teacher at the door, while Valerie stood, wide-eyed, staring at the transformed room. Decorated in a winter carnival theme, there was artificial snow everywhere. Trees were frosted with snow and icicles. An old sleigh was decked with brightly wrapped packages.

"It's beautiful," she gasped as Carl escorted her to a table at one side.

"Doesn't look like the same place where sweaty bodies stomp up and down throwing balls into hoops, does it?" He looked at Valerie then and smiled, his blue eyes searching hers. Her heart thumped. "Let me tie on the flowers." His fingers brushed her wrist, sending more electricity through her body.

"Carl!" A tall guy sauntered by. "Some chick. Introduce me?"

"Uh, Sam, this is Valerie Harding." Carl seemed reluctant to acknowledge Sam.

"I'm very glad to meet you, Valerie." He put a lot of emphasis on *very* and took her hand, holding it so long that Valerie had to pull it back.

"I may have to hang a sign on you that says, 'Carl's girl. Taken.' " Carl steered Valerie away from Sam and onto the dance floor. The band had started a slow number.

Carl's girl. Valerie liked the sound of it. She was so glad she'd taken the risk of going to the dance with him. It was worth anything that happened, any consequence she might have to suffer if her mother found out.

They danced every dance. Carl was a good dancer, a strong lead, sure of his steps. Valerie's natural grace made it easy for her to follow smoothly; and it was a delight to find a guy who liked to dance *and* was good at it.

But the evening was marred by two incidents. Sam came over about halfway through the evening and asked Valerie to dance. She looked at Carl and he nodded, reluctantly. So she stepped onto the floor with Sam.

He wasn't as good a dancer as Carl was, but he had a big smile and Valerie liked him. "You belong to Carl?" Sam asked softly in her ear.

"Of course not," Valerie responded automatically. "I don't belong to anyone."

Sam laughed. "I'm glad to hear that. Does Carl know you feel that way?"

"It hasn't come up. I haven't been going with him long," Valerie admitted. *This is our first real date*, she said to herself.

The subject did come up when Valerie returned to Carl. "I don't like your dancing with anyone else, Valerie," he said as they spun around the dance floor again. He held her extra close.

"Well, I—" Valerie wasn't sure what to say.

"If you think I'm jealous, I am," Carl whispered. "I want to keep you all to myself."

He made it seem all right. He made Valerie want to belong to him—tonight anyway. She pushed out of her mind the twinge of anger she'd felt at first when he said, "I don't want you dancing with anyone else."

Valerie was very strong-minded. She'd always chosen her friends, her activities. She'd always done what she wanted to do. Often she made a special issue of it. When roller skating became the big fad at Columbine, Valerie bought a skateboard. She'd always wanted a skateboard even though her mom didn't want her to have one. "It's too easy to get hurt on a skateboard," her mother said. "Hey, we're all getting skates," Kristen had said. There was something in her—she didn't know where it came from—that made her go against the crowd, do something different when everyone else was being alike.

She didn't like dressing like everyone else. She'd rejoiced tonight because no one, not even the most popular and beautiful senior girls, had a dress like hers. In fact, a couple of them had leaned over and whispered, "Great dress. Where'd you get it?" She was proud to say a friend made it.

Dori made a lot of Valerie's clothes. The rest she got in thrift shops, bargain basements, vintage-clothing stores. And she mixed and matched them in a style that was hers alone.

So Carl's telling her what to do rubbed her the wrong way. But she squelched her annoyance. If she had to, she'd tell him she didn't like his being that way. But not tonight. Not the first time they were together. She didn't want to spoil this evening.

But someone else almost did. The second incident happened in the girls' restroom. Valerie had just gone in when to her surprise, Lindsey Lewis, one of the most popular girls at Columbine Middle School, popped out of one of the stalls.

"Valerie Harding!" Lindsey looked surprised. "Does your mother know her baby is out? And with the big boys?" She laughed and washed her hands, then fluffed her hair. Then she leaned forward over the basin toward the mirror to apply lipstick.

Valerie tightened her fists but said nothing. A slight panic rushed through her before she could stop it.

That was just a saying—does your mother know you're out? Lindsey could have no idea that Valerie's mother would kill her if she did know she was there. If Lindsey found out, though, Valerie was sure she'd use the secret against her. Valerie was sure her mother would probably receive an anonymous letter by the next day's mail delivery. Lindsey was also one of the snottiest girls in their class.

"I suppose Dori Fiedler made your dress," Lindsey commented. Everyone at Columbine knew what a genious Dori was with a sewing machine.

"Yes, she did." Valerie ran a comb through her hair. Why was she standing here listening to Lindsey?

"I got mine at Irene's." Lindsey named the most exclusive dress boutique in town. Her dress was a froth of chiffon and taffeta ruffles, but made Lindsey look almost plump, if the truth be known.

Valerie borrowed her mother's way of responding, with a minimum of expression. "That's nice." She kept fumbling in her purse, not wanting to walk out with Lindsey. Taking out her mascara, she rolled it over her lashes carefully.

Finally Lindsey left. "See ya," she called over her shoulder.

I hope not, Valerie thought. Lindsey had forced her to think of her mother, and she'd promised herself she wouldn't do that the whole evening. Sighing deeply, Valerie took one last look at the image in the mirror, the make-believe star she'd become for one night. She went back to Carl, who grabbed her arm.

"There you are. I thought I'd lost you."

"No way." Valerie smiled at him and went back to her make-believe.

By the time they left the dance, Valerie was sure Carl was the only guy for her. She would never complain about his wanting her to be his girl exclusively. It had been the most wonderful evening of her entire life.

In the car outside Dori's, Carl pulled her toward him. "I've decided I do want to put you in my act, Valerie. I watched a famous magician on a TV special the other night. He has an assistant—and she wasn't even as beautiful as you. It gave me some good ideas. When can you practice?"

"I—I don't know." Valerie couldn't think about tomorrow. She wanted to think only of this moment—now.

"I'd call you, but I don't have your phone number. Surely after tonight you feel it's safe to give it to me?" He teased her lightly, then bent over and kissed her ear, her cheek.

She would have given him a dozen phone numbers, if she could remember any. "I . . . I . . . Can I call you tomorrow, Carl?" She had to decide how to handle his calling her, but right now she didn't want to think about the problems it might bring.

He laughed. "Secretive, aren't you?"

"I guess so."

Putting his hand on her chin, he tipped her mouth up to his and kissed her. She had never imagined how wonderful it would be. She wished she didn't have to go inside. Three girls were going to want to know everything, and she wanted to be alone.

She wanted to think of nothing but Carl Bentson, Carl the Magnificent, the most magnificent thing that had ever happened to her.

Chapter 5

Valerie let herself into Dori's house with the key Dori had given her; and to her surprise and relief, found Kristen, Sunny, and Dori asleep. Very quietly she placed the heels she'd slipped off at the door beside her overnight case. Then she slid out of the dress and hung it in Dori's closet. She snuggled down into her sleeping bag, mentally reliving the events of the night before falling fast asleep.

"Hey, we went to sleep before Cinderella came in!" Kristen came awake like a shot echoing across the quiet of the Christmas Eve morning. "Wake up, gang! Cinderella is here." Kristen shook Valerie's shoulder.

"Oh, no," groaned Valerie. She didn't want to get up yet. She didn't want to be awake.

"Get ice," yelled Sunny, another early riser.

Dori, who also didn't rise and shine, moaned along with Valerie. "Who let the cheerleaders loose?" She sat up and rubbed her eyes.

"What happened last night?" Kristen practically shouted. "Tell us what happened. Oh, pooh, I meant to stay awake. What time did you get in, anyway?"

Valerie gave up. "Just after midnight. I didn't want to turn into a pumpkin." Valerie smiled, remembering.

"Well, come on, don't just lie there grinning." Kristen poked Valerie. "Tell us what happened."

Valerie turned on her stomach and propped herself up on two elbows. "It was wonderful."

"So. The details, lady, the details." Kristen was getting frustrated.

"The gym was fantastic, like a winter wonderland. We had our pictures taken in the sleigh. We danced every dance but one, and Carl got jealous because his friend, Sam, asked me to dance, and he wants me to be in his magic show for sure, and we have to start practicing so I'll probably have to spend a lot of time with him."

"All right!" Kristen shouted. She was almost satisfied. "Did he kiss you good night?"

Sunny laughed at Kristen. "Could facing your mother's interrogation be any worse, Valerie?"

"Not much." Valerie grinned at her friends. "What do you think?" she said to Kristen.

"Ohhhhhh!" Kristen pretended to faint into her sleeping bag. "Why me? Why me?" she shouted. "I'm the only one who doesn't have a love in my life. I think I'll starve myself to death."

"Well, that's the answer." Valerie stretched and yawned, fully awake now, remembering the evening before. "If you lose twenty pounds, you might get some guy's attention."

"If I go to all the trouble and work to lose twenty pounds, it'll be for myself, not for some guy. The guys can love me the way I am or not at all." Kristen snapped.

"Good for you, Kristen." Dori came slightly awake. "Will someone who's more steady on her feet go put the teakettle on?"

"I will." Sunny jumped up. She always got up early. "Shall we have fudge or chocolate chip cookies for breakfast?"

"Ugh." Kristen wrinkled her nose and ran her hands through her mop of curls. "Even *I* can't go for that."

Dori's mother appeared at the bedroom door. "You girls awake? Your father says he'll take all your friends to breakfast, Dori. Unless you'll settle for cocoa and the big bag of croissants, sticky buns, and sweet rolls we just picked up at the French bakery." Mrs. Fiedler looked exhausted from the long hours she put in the day and night before, but she had a big grin on her face.

"Croissants?" Kristen fainted again.

"Who's babysitting Oscar?" asked Sunny. Oscar was the gorilla the Fiedlers were teaching to communicate in sign language. Someone had to be with him almost full time.

"We have one student who couldn't get home for Christmas. She's there now. We'll include her in our Christmas, and take turns babysitting Oscar this weekend."

The four girls put on their bathrobes and followed Mrs. Fiedler downstairs to the kitchen where Mr. Fiedler had a big fire roaring in the fireplace.

"Look!" squealed Valerie, running to the window. "Snow—snow for Christmas!"

A blanket of white softened the landscape of Heather Ridge, the subdivision where the girls lived. Yards looked like picture postcards from Victorian times.

"I knew they said it was possible, but I never dared hope." Sunny ran to look out.

"It makes the holiday perfect." Valerie sighed. "Just perfect."

"Did you tell us everything?" Kristen whispered, nudging Valerie. "I'll bet you edited out all the good parts."

Valerie hugged Kristen. "Would I do that?"

"Yes," the three girls said together. Mr. and Mrs. Fiedler looked puzzled.

"Have I told you how wonderful I think it is that you four are such good friends?" Mrs. Fiedler put her arm around Dori. She was as tiny as her daughter. Valerie could see the love between them.

A sharp stab of sadness hit her. If only she and her mother could be friends, share things. If only her mother wouldn't act like such a dictator, a prison guard, keeping Valerie locked up, or rather, letting her out on a short leash only to pull her back the minute Valerie went too far.

She pushed the thought away and gathered around the big table in the Fiedler kitchen, digging through the four white bags that Mr. and Mrs. Fiedler had brought from the bakery.

"Ummmm, they're still warm," Valerie said, pulling out a sticky bun laden with syrup and pecans.

"I've found the secret for entertaining teen-agers,"

Mr. Fiedler said as he laughed. "Feed them."

"That's no secret." Kristen said, nibbling the tip off a croissant.

The pastries disappeared quickly. The girls sat in front of the fire with mugs of hot chocolate, quietly watching the flames and thinking their own thoughts about the morning. Valerie loved the coziness, the warmth that came not only from the fire but from Dori's family and her friends' love.

Finally Mrs. Fiedler broke the spell. "When you're ready to go home, girls—and I'm not hurrying you— I'll drive each of you to your door. If you're anything like Dori, none of you wore boots."

I wore blue slippers, thought Valerie. Cinderella had worn blue, sparkling high-heel slippers to the ball. But Carl didn't turn into a pumpkin or a frog or one of his white rabbits. Valerie felt as if she had turned into someone else. She was a girl that a guy was crazy about, and it felt wonderful.

Suddenly, she wished she didn't ever have to go home. But she did, and to a mother who'd question her more thoroughly than Kristen did. Except, fortunately, her mother didn't know what questions to ask.

Chapter 6

To Valerie's surprise, her mother didn't ask many questions, and the questions she did ask were easily answered. "Who brought you home? I didn't recognize the car." Her mother quickly let down the pretense that she'd casually been sitting in front of the fire all morning. Valerie knew she'd been watching out the window for Valerie to come in.

"Mrs. Fiedler. They were home for a change."

"You mean they're not home when you spend the night over there?" Her mother jumped right on that possibility.

"*One* of them always is," Valerie fibbed quickly. "They do research at the university and one has to stay with the gorilla."

"Gorilla?" The word did what Valerie hoped it would. Her mother was distracted. "What are they doing with a gorilla?"

"Teaching it sign language—to communicate with humans." Valerie stood in front of the fire crackling in the family room fireplace, thinking that if she gave her mother a few minutes now, she could get by with spending the rest of the day alone in her room.

"I've worked with some tough bosses, but I guess that's better than working with a gorilla." Her mother laughed. Still dressed in a lounging robe, she pulled an afghan back over her legs. "Did you bake all evening as you planned?"

"We made a ton of cookies and fudge, but I didn't bring any home, Mom." Valerie sort of told the truth. "I didn't want to eat a lot of sweets all weekend. Besides Dori and Sunny packed up a lot of them to give to their boyfriends."

"That's nice." Her mother used her stock comment when she didn't want to say much. She opened the book she was reading, dismissing Valerie.

"Mom, Dori and Sunny are dating eighth-grade boys. What if I met a nice guy that I liked? What would be the harm in my double dating or triple dating with Sunny and Dori?" Valerie tested the waters, thinking her mom might be persuaded to give a little on her no-dating policy.

"Valerie, I don't think fourteen-year-old girls are ready to date. Now, if Mrs. Keifer and Mrs. Fiedler want to let their girls go with boys, that's their business, but you know how I feel. When you're sixteen, if I think you've met a nice boy, we'll see about some dating."

"Mom, at sixteen, I'll be ancient. Some of the girls have been dating since fifth grade."

"I don't want to hear what some of the girls are doing. You're not just one of the girls, Valerie. You're special. I care about you. You're all I have. I'm not going to let you go wild, never knowing where you are or whom you're with. And furthermore, if Sunny and Dori are going with boys, maybe you shouldn't run around with them either. They'll be bad influences on you."

Valerie was treading on dangerous ground. If her mother refused to let her see her friends, if she had to sneak around to be with Sunny and Dori, too, she didn't know what she'd do. The whole idea of it, her mother's narrow-minded thinking, made Valerie's stomach tighten and her whole body feel like a balloon stretched to the point of exploding.

"I'm not a baby any longer, Mother!" Valerie exploded. "I can't believe you're so narrow-minded." She flew out of the room and up the stairs. Slamming the door of her bedroom, she threw herself across her bed and pounded her pillow.

Next thing she knew her mother would decide a home tutor was safer. After all, Valerie shouldn't go to school since everyone there was a bad influence on her. Ever since she was a little girl, Valerie had heard, "Be careful crossing the street." "Don't play on the monkey bars, Valerie. You could get hurt." "Call me the minute you get to Kristen's (or Dori's or Sunny's) so I'll know you got there all right." Why hadn't she filled Valerie's room with cotton batting and locked her in it for eighteen years so she couldn't get hurt?

Valerie's anger no longer turned to tears as it had when she was younger. Maybe it went into that hard knot inside her that made her snap at people when they crossed her. The karate workouts eased some of it but she couldn't go in until Saturday. The studio was closed today and tomorrow. She could practice in her room, but she never enjoyed that as much.

Flicking on her radio to her favorite station, Valerie lay on her bed and listened to the music for a few minutes. Then, glancing at her bedside clock, she wondered if Carl was home. She'd feel better if she talked to him, made sure he was still out there, still real. Last night had been real.

She wished she had a phone in her room as Sunny did. She hated to risk her mother's hearing anything she said.

Sliding into slippers, Valerie walked softly back downstairs. Her mother was still in the family room reading; in fact, she had a stack of new romance novels at her side. Was that her plan for Christmas day and the weekend? Read about romance, but deny that it could happen to her or anyone else—especially her daughter?

As far as Valerie knew, her mother had never dated in all the years since her dad had left. Sometimes Valerie wanted to ask her mother about it, but it was a risky subject. Her mother was attractive but any talk of men brought out a bitter tone in her voice. Did she hate all men because of Valerie's father? Did she want to teach Valerie to distrust and hate men? It wasn't working.

Valerie decided to take a chance on using the phone in her mother's bedroom. Its distance from the family room afforded the privacy not possible with the kitchen phone.

Mrs. Harding's room was done in cream and peach. The curtains and bedspread were peach satin and lace and the furniture was a delicate French Provincial style, but there were Oriental touches here and there. An expensive Japanese screen covered with peacocks and swirls of leaves and flowers set off two big chairs and a glass-topped table. Valerie had never seen her mother eat there or have tea there, and she certainly never invited any guests there. If one of her women friends from work came over, they stayed in the kitchen or family room.

Valerie sat on the floor beside her mother's bed, the sleek, cream-colored phone in her lap. She had Carl's number memorized. She punched it in. It rang four times. *Be home, please be home, Carl*. He was and he answered, out of breath.

"Carl, did I disturb you?" Valerie asked, loving the sound of his voice.

"Valerie, hi. I was in my practicing room over the garage. I just came in. One of these days I'll get a phone out there. How are you? I enjoyed the dance. You looked wonderful. You're a good dancer, too."

That's what she needed to hear. "Thanks, Carl. I had a great time too. I called to give you my number, but my mother doesn't like me to be on the phone much. She's kinda funny that way." Valerie laughed, hoping Carl would take lightly the excuse she was making for her mother. "She hasn't really joined the electronic age yet."

"But phones have been around for an awfully long time."

"*I* know that. *You* know that." Valerie laughed again. "Anyway, it would be best if you only called me after school and before six." Would Carl suspect what was going on? He was no dummy. Valerie practically held her breath.

"Whatever you say, Babe. Just so I can talk to you some and see you a lot. Want to work on the act today? This afternoon?"

"I'd love to, but my mom has the day off. We

thought we'd go shopping, maybe eat out tonight." Valerie lied carefully, making it sound as if she and her mother were close and wanted to have some time together. That might balance out the idea of her mother's not liking her to be on the phone. Valerie could see that this was going to get complicated and take all the acting skills that she could summon.

"Then Saturday? Can you come over on Saturday? We could practice, go get a hamburger, then go to the movies."

How she wanted to say a plain yes. Instead, she ventured, "Well, I can practice some, but I don't know about a movie. Can I tell you Saturday?"

Valerie didn't think she was going to get by with saying she was spending the night with someone every Saturday night, maybe Friday too. Would Carl get tired of a girl he couldn't go out with all the time?

"Valerie? Who are you talking to? Why didn't you use the phone in the kitchen?" Her mother had come into the room.

"I have to go now," Valerie said to Carl suddenly. "Sorry, I'll call you back."

Her mother didn't seem angry, just puzzled.

"Girl talk, Mom. I was talking to Sunny. We thought we might do something Saturday night." Valerie lied again. It was getting easier. "Do we have any plans for Saturday night? Sunny thought the four of us might go to The Speak for hamburgers. Then Mrs. Keifer would give us a ride to the movies. I'd be in by ten-thirty or eleven."

"We'll see, Valerie. I wish we could have gone away for a few days. The holidays are always a little depressing."

"They wouldn't have to be, Mom." Valerie took the plunge. "Aren't there any nice single lawyers at the firm? I don't understand why you never go out. Kristen's mother remarried right away after her husband died, and she had three children at the time. Now she's got two more. Mr. McDowell is a great guy. He'd have to be to put up with that mob."

"I don't want to go out with anyone, Valerie. I tried it a couple of times and I was bored. Men are all the same."

Valerie wasn't ready for a lecture on sex. "I think you're wrong about that, Mom, but it's your life." Valerie got up and practically ran to her room, shutting the door.

Her mother's love life wasn't Valerie's problem but her own love life was. And as complicated as it got, Valerie vowed to keep seeing Carl.

Chapter 7

S ome snow remained on the ground on Christmas morning; but the sun was shining, and the snow was melting fast. Valerie and her mother slept late, then took cups of tea and plates of sweet rolls into the family room. Her mother had decorated a tiny tree in all blue ornaments and lights. She'd done it for Valerie's sake, Valerie knew.

When Valerie left home for good, her mom would probably stop celebrating holidays altogether. It was a thought Valerie didn't like. She didn't want to feel sorry for her mother but her mom was going to grow old all by herself and be very lonely someday—if she wasn't already. If she was ever lonely now, she hid it well—working long hours, staying busy around the house on Sunday, cleaning, watching television, and reading.

Valerie had bought her mom a lot of little presents: stationery, perfume, scarves, and earrings. As they exchanged gifts, Valerie reluctantly opened her presents from her mother. Her mother never accepted Valerie's taste in clothes, buying instead what she thought Valerie should be wearing. But Valerie had made a short list and stuck it on the refrigerator with a magnet. Usually her mom got her a few things on her list.

The first present was an inexpensive watch, an item that had been on Valerie's list. "Oh, thanks, Mom. It's great."

"Did you lose the watch I got you for your birthday?" her mother questioned.

Valerie laughed, knowing her mother was going to think she was nuts. "No, I'm going to wear more than one. This one will be set on London time."

"Why in the world would you want to know the time in London?"

Her mom would never understand, so Valerie didn't try to explain. "Oh, it's just fun."

Her mother shook her head and watched Valerie unwrap more presents. "I got you some nice sweaters, Valerie, and two skirts. If you just hate them, you can exchange them."

"They're all pretty, Mom," Valerie said after unwrapping several packages. "But no one wears preppy any more."

"It's a classic style. Isn't classic always in style?" Her mother just didn't understand.

"Thanks, Mom." Valerie gave up explaining. "I appreciate everything you got me. Merry Christmas."

"Merry Christmas, Valerie." There was a note of sadness in her mother's voice. Valerie tried to ignore it.

"Want to go to a matinee? I'd like to go over to Kristen's for a little while, then we could catch the two-thirty movie."

"Sure. That would be fun, but do you have to run off right now?"

"In a few minutes. I want to see what Kristen got, and her little sisters are always so crazy on holidays. It'll be total chaos over there. Want to come along?" Valerie pretty much knew what her mother's answer would be but if her mom wanted to go to Kristen's, it would be OK.

"No, I guess I'll stay here where it's quiet. By the way, a card came from your father. I put it under the tree."

"Oh, thanks, Mom." Valerie went for the card with some reluctance. Slowly she slid her finger under the opening and ripped it open. It was a cutesy card, letting her know her father thought she was still seven or eight years old but there was a check in it for fifty dollars. The greeting said, "Best wishes, Dad." He couldn't even say, "Love." But then how could he love someone he didn't know?

"Did . . . did he say anything?" Valerie's mother asked.

"No, he just sent a check." Automatically, Valerie folded it and put it in the back pocket of her jeans.

"That's nice." Her mother picked up the book she'd left on the coffee table the night before. "Don't lose it."

"I won't lose it, Mother." Valerie clinked her cup back onto its saucer, hopped up, and ran for the stairs, shutting her bedroom door.

Quickly she traded her jeans for loose sweats and started to work out. Blanking her mind, she concentrated fully on her exercises. It took a full half hour of karate to rid herself of some of the feelings she didn't want to carry with her to Kristen's.

Kristen answered the door laughing. The background noise sounded like a schoolroom gone wild. "Come in, Valerie, if you can stand it."

"Have you called the riot squad?" Valerie laughed. This was just what she needed. Her mood changed immediately.

"My dad's threatening." Kristen led Valerie to the back of the McDowell house where a huge family room echoed with shouts and squeals.

"Valerie! Valerie!" Two voices screamed. Becky, ten, and Noel, twelve, each grabbed one of Valerie's hands.

"What did Santa bring you?" Becky winked in an exaggerated manner and pointed behind her hand to the youngest McDowell girl, Glennie, who was four.

"Yeah, Valerie, what did Santa bring you?" Glennie asked. She had chocolate spread across her cheeks and hugged a new talking bear. "Want to hear what Teddy can say?"

"Sure, Glennie." Valerie sat on the floor and Glennie flopped into her lap. "And look what Santa brought me."

Valerie held out her arm that sported three watches. "This one is set on London time, and this one for Hong Kong. This one is our time."

"Weird," said Becky. "Why would you want to know what time it is in Hong Kong? You going there?"

Valerie laughed and shook her head.

"I think it's neat," said Noel. "Can I borrow your

watch, Becky? I want to do that too."

"Careful what fads you set here, Valerie," whispered Kristen. "They worship you. Becky is even talking about taking karate."

"It'd be good for her. She probably has to fight to get attention around here."

"Who's fighting to get attention?" Mr. McDowell came into the room. "If anyone does, it's me. I'll bet your house is quiet, Valerie. How about trading with me for the rest of the day?"

"Fine with me, Mr. McDowell. In fact, Mom and I are going to the movie this afternoon. That'd give you at least two hours of peace and quiet."

"That's all I ask for." Kristen's father pretended to pass out on the couch. "Even ten minutes would be nice."

The minute Mr. McDowell sat down, Becky was on one side of him and Noel on the other. "Show me how this works," said Becky, handing him a camera. Glennie climbed into his lap before he could do anything. He nestled her and Teddy against his chest while he tried to open the camera. Glennie's thumb popped into her mouth, and she looked as if she might go back to sleep.

"How long have you been up?" asked Valerie.

Kristen yawned. "I think I stayed in bed till six-fifteen. We have a rule that no one gets up till six. Let's go to my room so we can hear each other talk."

"Six-fifteen? How awful," said Valerie, although she didn't think being part of Kristen's large family would be bad at all.

"I suppose you slept in?"

"Yeah."

"Was it just terrible?" asked Kristen, not having to explain to Valerie what she meant.

"Well, yes and no. Mom got me a stack of preppy clothes, but she did say I could exchange them. I got a check from my dad for fifty dollars. The card was signed, 'Best wishes.' "

Kristen nodded, understanding and asking no further questions. She changed the subject. "Look at my loot while I get dressed." Kristen was still wearing a woolly pink chenille bathrobe. "Let's go over to Sunny's before I lose it here."

"Hey, you got two guitar books," Valerie called while Kristen was brushing her teeth. "And what's this—country-and-western records? I didn't know you were into C&W." Valerie knew that Kristen played her guitar for the kids at the Brown Bear Preschool where she worked after school two days a week, but she hadn't known that Kristen liked country and western.

"Some of it," Kristen said, returning from the bathroom with a hairbrush. She tried to tug it through her curly hair. "I'd like to sing some of those sexy ballads. I can't stick with 'Eensy Weensy Spider' forever.

"You write such good kids' songs, though," Valerie reminded her. "I'd think you could eventually record some of those for the children's market."

"It's possible." Kristen pulled on a jean jacket over her red knit sweater. "Like my new sweater?"

"Love it. You look great in red. Wonder what Peter gave Sunny."

When they left the house and were hurrying toward Sunny's, Kristen asked, "Did your mom question you a bunch about Wednesday night?"

"Hardly at all. I guess I got away with it. But, Kristen, it's going to be awful trying to find ways to keep going out with Carl. He's already asked me out for Saturday night and I don't know how to arrange it. But I'm going to."

"You sure it's worth it, Valerie?" Kristen shook her head. "I can't imagine trying to go anywhere without my family's finding out."

"Well, you do have more inquisitors. But it's worth it, Kristen." Valerie shoved her hands deep into her jacket pockets. "Carl is wonderful. Mom is so unfair about guys and dating. If she had it her way I'd never even look at a guy."

"What if we lived on some planet where girls and boys were raised separately until they were sixteen or even eighteen, or worse yet, till it was time to get married? Wouldn't that be awful?" Kristen posed a grim possibility.

"I'd stow away on a spaceship going to Earth," Valerie assured her.

"I'll bet you would. You've got more nerve, Valerie, than any person I know. Does karate do that for you?"

"I don't think so, but it does give me confidence. I think karate helps me focus my energy. And it sure helps me get rid of a lot of anger."

Kristen didn't have to ask the source of Valerie's anger. There were some things good friends didn't have to ask about. They just understood.

"I don't think I have enough anger to chop a wet noodle."

"You don't have anything in your life *to* be angry

about, Kristen. Do you know how lucky you are?"

"No, remind me. I'm twenty pounds overweight and there are no men in my life and—"

"And I don't think you care about either." Then, for whatever the reason, a sudden curiosity about her father clicked into Valerie's mind. "Do you ever wonder, Kristen, who your real father and mother were? What they were like? Why your mother couldn't keep you?"

"Or didn't want to?" Kristen added. "Yeah, I wonder about that a lot. I don't want to, but I guess it's natural when you've been adopted."

"Do you think you'll ever try to find out?"

"I might, though, I guess I'd feel guilty doing it. My own family is so great. But to know my natural parents might get rid of some ghosts."

"Yeah. If I could meet my father again just one time—see what he's like—it would help. I'm curious."

"Why are we talking about this?" Kristen asked suddenly, gathering up a snowball to throw at Valerie.

"I don't know, Stupid. Who started it?" Valerie let fly a white missile, screamed, and ran past Sunny's back door.

Kristen started to knock, but saw Valerie armed again so she jerked the door open and quickly took refuge. "Sorry, Mrs. Kiefer. I was losing the war." Kristen tried to catch her breath and apologize for barging in at the same time.

Mrs. Kiefer laughed and finished turning French toast in an electric skillet. The aroma of vanilla filled the air. "Who's the enemy? No, let me guess. It's the

53 🙶

karate expert and she's changed weapons."

"Right." Kristen peeked back out the door. A snowball thumped against the frame. "Eeek! Peace, Val. There's food in here!" Kristen implored.

"The magic word." Valerie stomped her shoes before entering the kitchen. "You just now eating breakfast?"

"No, this is lunch, but I'm making plenty for guests. I suspected you two would be here soon. Go on up to Sunny's room. She's putting on a new sweater, and Dori's up there. But all of you come back down and eat." Mrs. Kiefer handed one of the Irish setters a bit of bacon.

"Hey, hey, hey," Dori squealed when Kristen and Valerie burst into Sunny's room, Valerie still chasing Kristen. "The gang's all here. Are you two feuding on a holiday?"

"Why should today be any different? Thanks for the funky bracelet, Sunny," Valerie remembered to say. "I love it."

The girls had exchanged wrapped presents after their Wednesday night at Dori's but had taken them home to put under their trees. Valerie's funds had been limited, but she'd given each of her friends a big scarf, to wear tied over a blouse, and two paperback novels apiece. She knew they would all read and exchange the books.

"What did Peter give you?" Kristen asked Sunny.

"A locket," answered Sunny, holding out a silver heart on a chain. "Now I have to get his picture from him somehow."

"I got a locket too." Dori pulled hers out of her blouse. "I think Peter and Roger shopped in the same place."

"I'll bet neither of them knew what to get, so they shopped together for support," Kristen said.

They laughed. Valerie, gazing off dreamily, wished she'd known Carl long enough to exchange presents, but the dance had been present enough. She didn't need anything to remind her of an evening of dancing with Carl, his arms around her.

"Hey, Valerie's left us," Kristen clowned. "I wonder where she's gone?" She punched Valerie, bringing her back to Earth.

"Listen, do you want something neat to think about?" Sunny said, flopping on her bed.

"Sure," said Kristen. "Tell us."

"There's going to a New Year's Eve party at the roller rink. Peter wanted to take me, but I said if all four of us could go, we'd meet the guys there. How about it?"

Valerie knew that Sunny had been thinking about Kristen when she made that plan. But Valerie could tell Carl to meet her there too. Great idea! And her mother might not argue about her going someplace with her three friends. After all, they went to the rink all the time.

It was something to think about, all right. And another chance to see Carl if she couldn't manage Saturday night. She'd go to the rink with the girls, but Carl could take her home. She'd have him drop her off at Sunny's, then walk home after he left. Or maybe the foursome could spend the night at Sunny's this time. Things were working out. It would take some patience on her part, and some faith, but she'd make it work.

Chapter 8

The rest of Christmas day wasn't too bad. Valerie and her mother saw a great movie, then stopped for pizza on the way home. Her mother made a joke about pizza for Christmas dinner, but Valerie had vetoed Furr's Cafeteria where her mother wanted to go. Furr's had great food, but Valerie couldn't stand the idea of going there for Christmas dinner.

Valerie spent the evening writing in her journal about Carl. To be sure her secret was safe, she gave him a code name and wrote in a kind of shorthand. Her mother probably never would find her journal, but if she did Valerie knew she'd read it. Valerie was taking no chances.

On Saturday morning she called Carl as soon as she got to the studio, catching him just before he left on an errand for his mother. "Two o'clock is fine, Valerie," he said. "Are the dinner and movie on?"

"Yes," Valerie said. She had told her mother she was going to the movie with her friends. She had to promise to be home at ten-thirty, but it was better than not going at all.

Luckily she had a locker at the karate school. She couldn't decide which sweater to wear, so she wore one and took the other in her bag along with her *gi*. She'd told her mother she'd be at the school all day, then go to eat and to the movie. She sure hoped there'd be no reason for her mother to call her at the studio. Mrs. Harding had never called before. It was as if her mother pretended Valerie's absorption in karate didn't exist.

Valerie had her own class on Saturday morning. She put all her nervous energy into the workout.

"Good job, Valerie," Al Warrington said to her halfway through the class. "Karate is a good sport for someone with your energy. And your ballet training put you right in there with conditioning, grace, and precision. A lot of people can't handle the discipline that karate demands."

Valerie tucked away the compliment to recall when she needed some positive strokes. Right now she was humming with good feelings about the rest of her day. She went back to the sparring practice, drawing Gary Yardley for a partner, since he was standing next to her when they paired off. She always had to spar with a guy—she was the only girl in the class. There'd been another girl in her brown belt classes but Carol had dropped out when her friends started teasing her too much. Valerie would certainly not let her peers influence her life like that.

"Ease off, Harding," Gary said. "You trying to show me up in front of my friends?" Gary was partly teasing, but Valerie had bested him several times already.

"Go home if you can't handle the heat, Gary." Valerie smiled.

"You're a real smart alec, Harding, you know

that?" Gary said. "I pity the guy who tries to go out with you."

"Maybe he'll have more guts than you do, Gary." Valerie threw a punch that narrowly missed giving Gary a black eye. "You going to have the guts to tell your friends how you got a shiner?"

All the guys teased Valerie. But the truth of the matter was that she could keep up with any of them, and they knew it. So while they might give her a bad time, they respected her.

Most of the guys in the class were older. Four were even seniors in high school, but for some reason Valerie had never thought of them as guys to go out with. She had been in class with a lot of them for the last three years, but they were more like brothers to her.

Keith McNally stopped her after class and said, "You looked really great at the Christmas dance, Valerie. I hardly knew it was you." Keith prepared to duck any punch Valerie could throw his way.

Valerie laughed instead. "I didn't see you. It was a wonderful dance, wasn't it? Someone worked really hard on decorations."

"How long have you known Carl Bentson?" Keith asked.

"Not long. Why?" Was Keith trying to tell her something or was he just curious?

"No reason. I've known him for a long time. He's a good magician."

Valerie started to tell Keith she was going to help Carl with his act, but she decided not to. Maybe the fewer who knew the better.

"Going to help with classes today, Valerie?" Mr.

Warrington interrupted her.

"This morning—till noon." Valerie waved to Keith and followed Al to where he was starting the Pee-Wee class, kids five years old. They were so cute that Valerie loved working with them.

The morning flew by with no more time to think about Carl. Valerie usually went home without showering, but at noon she slipped into the small room she had been given as a dressing room and rinsed off under a stream of hot water. Pulling on her jeans, she decided on the olive green sweater. She took her hair from its pony tail and brushed it till she was satisfied with the way it looked.

"Here I come, Carl, ready or not," she whispered, and bounced out of the studio.

Carl lived about a mile north of Heather Ridge. It was a good walk, but the sandwich Valerie had wolfed down before she started walking seemed to be gone by the time she got to his neighborhood. She was starving. She hoped that Carl would offer her something to eat.

The homes in Carl's neighborhood weren't as expensive as those in hers but the profusion of large, old trees suggested it was an old neighborhood. Carl's house was a modern ranch with a small garage at the back of the driveway. Valerie guessed that the window at the top was Carl's studio.

She swallowed her case of nerves and rang the bell. This felt different from Carl's picking her up at Dori's. Maybe it was only that she didn't have her trio of friends backing her up.

"Hi, you're a little early," Carl said, opening the door.

"I'm sorry. Is it OK? I finished with the classes and came on over. I can come back."

"No, no, it's fine. Did you have any lunch?"

"A little. I—"

"Good, we can go to work then. Mom dropped me off. We ate in town after some shopping, then she went back to the store."

Where was Mr. Bentson? Was she alone with Carl? How silly of her. She told herself it would be all right if she were alone with him. In fact, Carl didn't even invite her into the house.

"Let's go on out to the garage. I need some practice badly. I had two shows over the holiday, so I didn't keep up my schedule of learning new tricks and polishing old ones."

The room over the garage was bigger than Valerie had expected. The ceiling sloped down on both sides, but it didn't take away from the space since it was so steep. Boxes, stacked up on a table and holding props for tricks, were carefully labeled and filed in alphabetical order. Valerie was amazed at Carl's organization. She felt that she shouldn't dare touch anything without permission.

"I've made a list of tricks where I can use someone to hand me something or hold something for me. Let's practice those first."

Valerie got less and less worried about being alone with Carl. He acted as if he had hired her to help, or as if he'd never seen her until today. There was none of the romance of the Christmas dance. Carl was all business.

He showed Valerie where to stand and what to hand him first, then he got started. He ran through several tricks, carefully putting away the props after each one, then getting props out for the next. Valerie was starting to get tired of watching him, when he said, "Let's take a break. Want a soda?" He went over to a small, square brown fridge in one corner of the room. Valerie hadn't noticed it.

"I'd love one," she said, gratefully sinking into a chair.

"Keith McNally says you're in his karate class. First class for black belt. Isn't that pretty high? I didn't know you did karate."

"There are ten degrees of black belt," Valerie told him. "I figured everyone knew I did karate. I get teased about it a lot." She couldn't tell if it bothered Carl for her to be good at the sport.

"I guess I don't know a lot about you," Carl said, and smiled. The smile helped Valerie relax a little. She didn't know what was wrong, but she was beginning to think this was a different person from the one she'd gone out with. "Can you really break boards?"

"Yes, but breaking boards is only a small part of karate. We do that in the demonstrations because that's what people expect to see. It gets their attention."

"Does it hurt your hand?"

"Only if you don't break the board," Valerie explained patiently. "The trick is concentration."

"Oh, then it is a trick. You use trick boards."

"No, I didn't mean a trick like you're doing. I meant the secret of my success. I focus in my mind. I see my hand going through the board."

Carl got quiet, as if he didn't know what else to

say. Valerie sipped her drink and wished Carl had some chips or popcorn, anything to eat. She was starving. She resisted the temptation to look at her watch—she'd worn only one. Today she had dressed pretty conservatively—for her.

"Well, back to work. You need to work with more of a flourish, Valerie, like this." Carl bowed to Valerie and swept a cardboard tube through the air. He would pull scarves from it. "This is show business."

"Is my only purpose to stand here and hand you things?"

"And look pretty." Carl smiled. "I'm doing the tricks."

"I thought you'd teach me some things." Valerie was getting one of her energy surges, making it almost impossible for her to stand still. Only the morning's exercise had kept her quiet this long.

"It takes a long time to learn most of these tricks. I'm out of the easy ones. Are you bored?"

"Oh, no," Valerie lied quickly. But she was, even though she'd never say so. She'd thought that being with Carl would keep her entertained, but he was different somehow. Maybe he was so used to working alone that he forgot she was there. Forgot she was there! She was not a person to forget about. How could anyone forget she was around? And did she want to be with a guy who forgot she was there?

He hasn't forgotten, she told herself. He's concentrating. It's like karate. You wipe out everything in your mind but the *kata*. You focus inward and on what you're doing.

Nonetheless, she wasn't used to being still for so long. She was tired and she wanted to do something else. She refused to believe she was bored with Carl, but she wanted him to relax, be the person he was at the dance. In a few minutes, she reassured herself, they'd go get dinner and go to the movies. They'd talk and get better acquainted and he'd be the guy he was at the dance.

Meanwhile, she took a deep breath and vowed to be patient.

Chapter 9

Valerie was ready to scream, or shout, anything to release her pent-up energy, when Carl finally said they had practiced long enough. Could she keep doing this? She didn't have to make a decision right then, she decided, so she put it out of her mind. She'd see how the evening went.

"Come and meet my family, Valerie," Carl said, leading the way out of the garage loft. "Then we'll go get something to eat. What movie do you want to see?"

Food was all Valerie could think about, but she told Carl about the movie that she and her mother had seen and suggested two others she thought she'd like.

Mr. Bentson looked like an older Carl. His skin was the same dark olive, his hair graying a little, but thick and curly.

"Glad to meet you, Valerie," he said. "Carl is lucky to have found such a beautiful assistant. You sure anyone will look at you, son?" Mr. Bentson's blue eyes teased.

Carl grinned. "I'm not going to worry. She'll make me look like a class act, and people will get used to her. Every magician has a cute assistant."

"I have plenty of chili made, Carl," Mrs. Bentson said after introductions were over. She was plump and cheery, dressed in a flowered housedress and a big apron. An old fashioned picture of a mother. "If you change your mind, you all can eat here."

The kitchen smelled of chili and homemade bread. Valerie wanted to grab up one of the crusty loaves cooling on the counter and run. She smiled to herself at the idea.

"I wish my mother baked bread," Valerie said. "It smells heavenly." She was out and out hinting. *How awful*, she thought.

"It's still warm." Mrs. Bentson ignored Carl. "Here, at least let me give you a piece, spread with butter. I know how young folks can eat." Mrs. Bentson grabbed a knife and a cutting board and sliced heavy, thick pieces. Smearing the heel with butter, she handed it to Valerie.

"Oh, thank you, Mrs. Bentson. It looks great. Maybe I should learn to bake." She knew she never would, but it was something to say as she sank her teeth gratefully into the moist, warm bread.

"I'll be glad to give you the recipe, Valerie. Making bread is easy."

Carl didn't refuse his slice, but he took it to the back of the house while he got ready for their date.

Valerie sat on a kitchen chair. "Your kitchen is so homey."

"I suppose your mother works like most women do today." Mrs. Bentson poured herself a cup of coffee and sat opposite Valerie at the formica-topped table. "I never have. Never wanted to. Seemed like

Carl and his sisters were enough work."

Carl had never mentioned any brothers or sisters. It turned out he had two sisters, but they were grown and married.

"Carl is our baby, Valerie." Mrs. Bentson smiled and sipped her coffee. "We've probably spoiled him. I hope you can put up with that."

"I'm sure I can." Valerie laughed. "I'm an only child, so I'm probably pretty spoiled myself."

"Another piece of bread?" Mrs. Bentson asked, as Valerie licked her fingers.

"Oh, no, thank you, but I'd better wash up."

Mrs. Bentson showed Valerie a bathroom off the master bedroom. She freshened up, washing her face and putting some lotion on, combing her hair, and rolling a little mascara on her eye lashes. She coated her lips with a slightly orange-tinted lip gloss. She wished she could brush her teeth, but hadn't thought to bring a toothbrush. If she was going to live away from home so much, she was going to have to carry a bigger purse and plan better.

"Ready, Val?" Carl called to her from the front of the house. "We need to leave." He put his arm around her shoulders to get her out of the house. "I don't like being late for the movie."

Valerie waved good-bye to Carl's parents who stood and watched them leave as if this were Carl's first date. She knew it wasn't. He was too natural, too smooth around her.

While they grabbed some tacos at a restaurant along the way, Carl ticked off the dates he had for performances. Valerie was surprised at how many he had. "I'm also working with a scout troup getting a magic badge, but I won't need you for that beyond the kick-off show."

"I think you'll have to write down the dates, Carl." Valerie crunched through a shell that held meat, lettuce, and tomatoes that were topped with cheese. She picked up every tiny flake of the shell with her fingertip before she started on a second. "I'll never remember them. And I might not be able to work every date."

"Why not?" Carl was still acting like a businessman.

"Well, I might have a class or a competition. And I spend a lot of time with Sunny, Kristen, and Dori."

"You can plan on spending a lot of time with me now." He smiled, and her heart pounded, making her want to spend a lot of time with him. Was he finally going to relax and make this more of a date than a business dinner? Maybe he was more nervous than he seemed. Maybe he covered being nervous with this business-like attitude.

"I'd like that." She smiled back.

"Every guy at the dance was jealous of me, being with you. You made me look good." Now Carl was saying things she would rather hear. Valerie's heart skipped a beat and she stopped being hungry.

"Want another?" He had noticed her appetite.

"No, I'm fine. Thanks."

He opened the car door for her, making her feel special again. This was more like a date, at last.

"There's another seatbelt in the middle," Carl said, looking at her and holding out his arm.

She scooted over near him, feeling a warm glow fill her.

In the line waiting to buy tickets at the movie, he put his arm around her casually, almost as if he were leaning on her. Valerie felt a little self-conscious then, but still she liked the closeness.

There was a huge crowd at the fourplex theater. The holiday weekend had brought everyone out. Valerie glanced around but didn't see anyone she knew. She'd like to double date someday with Peter and Sunny or Dori and Roger, but she'd wait until she and Carl had been going together longer. He seemed to like the two of them being alone.

The movie, a murder/romance, was scary. At first Carl took Valerie's hand, but then as the suspense mounted, he put his arm around her. She snuggled close.

The credits came on and they lingered. Valerie hated to end the warm feeling she had. "Ready?" he whispered.

"Sure." She got up and led the way up the aisle.

Suddenly, coming out of the dark and into the bright lights of the hall, Valerie looked up and blinked. Blinked again. Her whole body filled with a panic that demanded, Run! It was just as if the killer in the movie were following her late at night. She wanted to run yet she was frozen to the spot. But it was no killer coming toward her. It was her mother.

"Excuse me, Carl. I'll be right back." Ducking behind three women, Valerie melted into the crowd, then slipped into the ladies' restroom. She all but ran into a booth, fortunately empty, and clicked the door shut. What terrible luck! The last person she expected to see that night was her mother. Her mom had never said anything about going to another movie but, then,

Valerie hadn't been home all day. Ruth Berger had probably called her and, being lonely, she said sure.

How long should she hide? Not long. How long would it take her mother and Mrs. Berger to walk to their car? Then Valerie's stomach tightened even more. She heard a familiar voice.

"Wasn't he handsome, Ruth? It was a terrible plot, but who cares." Valerie's mother laughed and stepped into the stall right next to Valerie's.

Quickly Valerie slid as far as she could toward the other side of her cubicle. She looked down at her feet. Half the people in town wore black high-tops. Would they give her away? She decided she needn't worry. But the knowledge that only one thin wall separated her from her mother sent Valerie into near panic.

Where was Ruth? It would be stupid of Valerie to bolt and run. If Mrs. Berger wasn't in a stall, she'd recognize Valerie. That would be as bad as having her mother see her. Mrs. Berger would probably call out, "Grace, you'll never guess who's here. It's Valerie!" And Valerie would have to say hi to her mother. She could always say that Sunny, Dori, and Kristen were waiting for her outside, but maybe her mother would say, "Oh, I haven't seen them lately. I'll go say hi."

It was too late to run now. Valerie hadn't thought fast enough. And Carl was going to wonder where she was. He'd think she was sick or something was wrong. What was she going to tell him? That there was a line? That was it. She'd had to wait in line.

Waiting, Valerie practically got claustrophia in the tight booth. She listened while her mother took her time washing her hands and talking to Ruth. Valerie fought down the ball of fear that had risen from her stomach to her throat. Could you throw up from fear? If so, she at least was in the right place. *Come on, come on, Mother. Get out of here.*

Finally Valerie opened the door and peeked out, bending over, pulling up her socks at the same time. There was a line now, and a lady came and took Valerie's hiding place, impatient with her slowness at moving out.

Slowly Valerie washed her hands and dried them under the blower, twisting and rubbing them together in the warm air. Then she combed her hair and put on fresh lip gloss.

"What a line," she said to Carl, who was pacing the floor by the popcorn machine. "Sorry," she apologized.

Carl gave her a funny look, but said nothing. What could he say? Valerie felt embarrassed on top of the fear that still hadn't gone away. If she did this again, she'd choose a movie that was way across town and beg Carl to see that one. The trouble was that in the malls around Heather Ridge there were about ten movie theaters. It would be hard to justify driving so far away just so that she wouldn't accidently run into her mother.

Valerie was so jumpy the rest of the evening— which wasn't long since she had to be home at ten-thirty—that she made Carl nervous. The romantic mood that had started to build during the film was gone.

"You OK, Valerie?" Carl asked as they neared Sunny's house.

Valerie had told him that Sunny's address was hers.

Kristen's house was closer but the yard was always full of toys and bikes and Carl knew she was an only child.

"Yeah, sure. Maybe the movie scared me more than I realized." She tried to joke about acting strangely.

"I'll protect you." He pulled her close and kissed her. But it wasn't the same as the Christmas kiss. Valerie had totally ruined any mood of romance. And her mind had never settled back on Carl completely. It was as if all she could think about was getting home quickly. Getting up to her room safely. She might even get home before her mom if they'd gone for a snack.

"When will I see you again? I need to give you a schedule too," Carl said before she got out. She'd already told him not to walk her to the door. She assured him that she wasn't really scared of a murderer. But to herself she thought that it was her mother who was much more likely to strangle Valerie.

"I don't know. Oh, yes, yes, I do. There's a New Year's Eve party at the roller rink. Want to go?"

"Yeah, sure. That'd be fun. What time can I pick you up?"

"Uh—well—the four of us girls planned to walk over together. I'll meet you there."

Carl was silent for a minute. "OK. I guess that's OK. See you then, unless we can get in another practice session before Thursday night."

Another practice session? What was there to practice? Valerie standing beside Carl, handing him things? Valerie wanted to be in Carl's magic show, but she didn't want to practice again.

"I'm pretty busy at the studio. I'll see you at the rink." She jumped out of the car, slammed the door, and ran toward Sunny's front porch. Once she turned and waved, in case Carl was watching. She hoped he didn't feel he had to see her actually enter the door. He didn't. She stopped and watched his car hum off down the street. Slowly she started the cold walk home.

This was dumb. It was really dumb. The whole afternoon, the evening had been filled with mixed emotions—part of them terrible, even scary. Part of them great. It was certainly not how dating had been in Valerie's dreams and fantasies.

Chapter 10

Valerie's mom called to her as she came in. "Hi, Valerie. Want some cocoa? Did you have a good time? What movie did you see? Ruth Berger and I ended up going to the movies too."

"Thanks for the cocoa, Mom, but I'm exhausted. May I be excused? It was a long day." That was no lie. It had been. So much had happened, and she needed to think. She would like something to eat, but she couldn't take any chances now. She'd sneak down later if she didn't fall right to sleep.

She slept, fitfully, and dreamed. Over and over she dreamed that she was being chased. The only details she could remember, though, had to do with a big box. She was huddled in the bottom of the box and all around the top edges, people peered in at her.

On Monday, Valerie spent the afternoon at the karate studio. She helped with classes, then took her own class, which was from five to six in the afternoon.

After class, Keith McNally surprised her. "Call

home, Valerie. Tell your mother you're going out to dinner and to a movie—with me. Want to? You know I won't make any moves on you," he teased. "I've felt enough of your punches." He rubbed the sore spot his arm had gotten when he hadn't countered fast enough while sparring with Valerie.

"Oh, Keith—thanks, but I can't. I have to go straight home.

"Are you going steady with Carl?" Keith asked.

"Of course not." Valerie didn't know why she said it so fast. She wouldn't mind going steady with him. But she didn't consider two dates going steady.

"OK, just checking. Some other time?" Keith smiled and Valerie didn't know why she hadn't noticed before how cute he was. His hair spilled over into his eyes because he needed a haircut, and his green eyes sparkled and teased her.

"Maybe—yeah, sure, Keith. I'm really busy with school and practice, though. Maybe we could have a soda after school sometime and walk over here together."

She hurried off toward home. Dating Carl seemed to have made other guys, like Keith and Sam, notice her. At least Sam hadn't called and asked her for a date. She was having enough trouble dating Carl in secret. No way could she start going out even more frequently.

What she was doing was like living a lie, where you have to tell another to cover the first. Soon it grew and grew until inevitably you got caught. But no way did she want to get caught. So she might have to pretend that she and Carl were going steady.

The phone was ringing when Valerie got home.

She ran to catch it, but her mother had come in, too, and she got to the phone first. Now Valerie was sure it was Carl, though she hoped it wasn't. What would she tell her mother? That she couldn't keep guys from calling her? It was normal for them to think she could date. Or that he wanted a homework assignment?

"For you." Her mother held out the kitchen extension. "It's Kristen."

Valerie relaxed and listened for Kristen's cheery voice.

"Valerie? Come over after supper. I'm getting cabin fever. I wish school had started today."

"Me too. I know what you mean." Valerie held the receiver against her stomach. "Can I go over to Kristen's after dinner, Mom?" Valerie made a big deal of asking permission so that her mother would never suspect that she'd do otherwise.

"I guess so." Her mother was rummaging in the refrigerator. "I should have stopped for groceries, but I was too tired. Today was a mess. Four days off almost isn't worth it."

"I don't mind eggs, an omelet," Valerie said, starting toward her room after telling Kristen she'd be over soon.

"I do. I had quiche for lunch," she heard her mother answer.

By the time Valerie had showered and returned downstairs, wearing her overalls and striped shirt, her mom had spaghetti boiling and some sauce heating. She had half a loaf of French bread in the microwave, thawing it out. "You can start a salad, Valerie."

"OK, Mom." Was her mother in a good mood? Valerie couldn't tell. She knew her mother was tired, but so was she. She had worked out with every class through the day and then sparred a lot during her class. For once it was easy to sit still.

Halfway through the meal, she said, "Mom, there's a party at the skating rink on New Year's Eve. The girls are going. Do you mind if I go too? We might spend the night at Sunny's."

"I don't want you out on New Year's Eve, Valerie. Too many drunk drivers. Too many crazies."

"It's not that far to drive. And Mrs. Keifer will probably take us and pick us up. Please don't say no. I can't stay home on New Year's Eve."

"I guess I will. There's a party after work at the office. Then Ruth and some of the other singles are going someplace. But if it's a bar, I'd rather come home."

Her mother's plans weren't the issue. Valerie kept eating, giving her request time to sink in. Her mother usually gave in after some initial protest against whatever Valerie wanted to do. That is, after first listing all the horrors that might happen, and an interrogation of whom she'd be with.

"I'll ask Kristen if her mother is letting her go. If so, we can go over together. We could walk. It's not far."

"I don't want you out walking at midnight."

"I meant *over* there. Not home. Someone will bring us home." Carl would bring her home, she knew.

"I guess a bunch of boys will be over there."

"Mother, of course, some guys will be there skating. Half of Columbine Middle School will be there. There probably won't be room to skate. But I go to school with boys, Mom. It's normal." Valerie had to be careful not to say too much.

"I don't know why I've ever let you go to the roller rink. Roller rinks always have a bunch of hoodlums hanging out."

Surely her mother wouldn't say no. If their house had a tower, Valerie bet her mother would lock her in it. "Valerie, Valerie, let down your hair," the prince, Carl, would call from below. And Valerie would uncoil her long, long braids for the prince to climb up. Even locking Rapunzel in the tower hadn't kept her from meeting a prince. Hadn't Valerie's mother read that story?

"Valerie, your father called me at work today." Her mother's voice tightened as she spit out the words quickly. "He's moving to Boulder, getting a new job at the university. He's decided he wants to see you."

Valerie didn't know what to think. "Should . . . should I see him?" she stammered. Her mother would have an opinion.

"I can't stop him from seeing you. The courts gave him permission. He just never wanted to." Now her mother sounded bitter.

Was that true? Her father had lived in Michigan. Maybe it was too far to come. Maybe he wished he could see her, but never got a chance.

"I'm not going to let you go and live with him, you hear. He would just let you run wild. He wouldn't care what you did." Once again, her mother failed to answer the question directly. She still didn't know if she *should* see her father.

"Mom, I don't want to go live with him. I don't know him. I'm not even sure I want to *see* him." But Valerie thought she did, out of curiosity, if nothing

77 &

else. What was wrong with her mother, thinking Valerie would hop up and go live in Boulder with her father? She didn't want to leave her school, her friends. Go live with a stranger. Did her mother really think she might do that? She'd have to be nuts.

"When would this be—that he'd want to see me?"

"Maybe next week. He already has a place in Boulder. He came out at Thanksgiving and found a house for his family. They have to be here by mid-January to start the semester."

"Why didn't you tell me?" Valerie pushed the last of her spaghetti around on her plate.

"I didn't think it would change anything. I never dreamed he'd want to see you after all this time."

"Maybe he's curious. He wants to see if I have two heads or if I'm really ugly, or something." Valerie tried to joke. This was painful.

"He's never cared before," her mother reminded her acridly. She got up to rinse her plate and put it in the dishwasher. Then she stood, staring out the kitchen window, even though it was dark and she couldn't see anything.

"I'm going over to Kristen's. I'll only stay about an hour."

"Your friends could spend the night over here sometime, Valerie. Don't you ever invite them?"

"I . . . I . . . sure, I'll tell them." It wasn't a good time to tell her mother that she didn't want to invite her friends to spend the night with her. She wanted to escape to their houses. That's what she was doing. She knew it. Escaping—and she was getting to be an expert at it. It had gotten to be a way of life, so much so, that she rarely thought about it. And her friends never questioned why Valerie didn't invite them to her house. They knew Valerie thought her mother was impossible.

Grabbing a jacket, Valerie ran all the way over to Kristen's. She was almost sick to her stomach by the time she got there, but didn't realize it until she'd rung the bell.

"Are you all right?" Kristen asked, opening the front door.

Valerie sat on the porch, her head between her knees. "Maybe. My spaghetti didn't like the bouncing I gave it. I ran without thinking of the consequences."

Kristen sat beside her on the step. She put her arm around Valerie. "Is that all?"

"No, but you're going to freeze. Let's go inside and talk. I think I'm OK."

"Wanna play Ping-Pong, Valerie?" Noel asked. "We can play partners. I get you, and Kristen and Becky can be together."

"You and Becky play, Noel," Kristen said. "Valerie and I want to talk."

"Talk-talk-talk. That's all you ever do. Maybe I don't want to be a teenager after all. It sounds boring."

Kristen and Valerie laughed. "It's anything but boring," Valerie whispered to Kristen. "Wait till you hear the latest."

"Want something to drink? A soda?" Kristen offered before they sought the sanctuary of her room.

When Kristen's oldest sister, Maggie, had gotten married, Kristen got her room. The oldest got some privacy, her mother had decreed. Kristen had celebrated for days. She'd been rooming with Noel, and much as she loved her sisters, she needed a little breathing room. Valerie was amazed at how well all the McDowells got along together. Kristen spent a lot of time with her sister and her sister's new baby, and she worked at Glennie's preschool.

"What's up?" Kristen asked, as soon as the door was closed.

Kristen's new record was on, and the two had flopped on pillows on the floor in front of the stereo.

"You'll never guess." Valerie sipped her drink and her stomach stopped churning. "My father is moving to Boulder, and he wants to see me. Next week, maybe."

"Well, that's a new wrinkle. Scary, isn't it?"

"Sure is. My mom's having a cow. You know what she said? She's worried that I'll decide to go off and live with him. I'd never do that. As bad as it is at home, I'm used to it. And I don't even know my dad, much less his wife."

"You may have a lot of half-brothers and sisters," Kristen said. "You may be just like me and have four sisters." She doubled over laughing.

"I never thought of that. I hope not. Mom never mentioned it." Valerie grinned at the idea. Was it possible? It didn't matter, she wasn't going to live with them. But it was funny to think about.

"At least this took Mom's mind off New Year's Eve. I think she'll let me go to the rink. You're going, aren't you?"

"I don't know, Val. You three guys are going to have dates there. I think I'll feel funny."

"Nonsense. We're going together, coming home together. Maybe we can spend the night at Sunny's.

And there'll be lots of guys there without dates."

"You're a traitor, Val," Kristen half teased. "I knew your mother had said you couldn't date, and no guys have asked me, so I figured you and I would stick together. Now you're sneaking around to see Carl, and I'm feeling left out." Kristen had stopped teasing.

Valerie spilled the news of the near tragedy on her second date with Carl. She made the episode funny to joke Kristen out of her blues. It worked. Kristen was never down for long. Soon both were laughing.

It felt good. Valerie realized she hadn't done much laughing during the last week. Her life was getting much too intense. Carl seemed to be two people, the businessman and the romantic prince. She wanted only one in her life. Keith McNally had decided she was a girl after all. They'd always been just friends at the karate school. If she wasn't so crazy about Carl, she might enjoy running around with Keith.

And now on top of all that, her father was putting in an appearance after ten years of sending cards that said, "Best wishes." Was her mother on the right track after all? Was life easier without men? And was it only a couple of weeks ago that Valerie's wildest dream was getting a date with someone at the high school? She had been the one of the foursome who spent all her time looking over the available guys and she had enjoyed flirting with the guys that did come around them.

All of a sudden her life was in the biggest mess it had ever been. And who was to blame? Guys.

"Guys! Bah, humbug," she said aloud.

"Valerie! I don't believe I heard you say that. You

don't really mean it, do you?" Kristen's face lit up with a huge smile. Then she started to laugh out loud and soon she was doubled over with laughter.

"It's not funny, Kristen. It's not funny."

Chapter 11

For the next three days, Valerie put everything out of her mind but her karate lessons, working out at the studio, and helping with classes. And, of course, the New Year's Eve party. Her mother had never said yes, but she hadn't said no either. If that happened, Valerie intended somehow to do as she pleased. But it was as if her mother were realizing she couldn't always keep Valerie from doing things that her friends were doing. It was a time her mother probably would have liked to say no, but since she thought Valerie was going with Kristen, Sunny, and Dori, she seemed to be hesitating to do so.

Late Thursday afternoon, with an invitation from Kristen for dinner and one from Sunny for spending the night, Valerie left her mother a note. "Going to Kristen's for dinner. We'll go straight to the skating rink and then Mrs. Kiefer is coming with the car at midnight. See you tomorrow. Happy New Year!" Valerie had worded the note so she never said she was riding home with Mrs. Kiefer, just that Mrs. Kiefer was going to be there with her car.

She had also called Carl, just to touch base, and to remind him of the evening. Could he forget? "We'll be there at eight, Carl," Valerie said. "I can hardly wait to be with you. I've missed you." Valerie wondered if she were being too forward, but she wanted Carl to know how she felt about him. She had been distracted when they had parted the time before, and Carl might take that to mean she didn't care about him.

And she did miss him. She found herself filled with the same nervous and excited anticipation she'd had before the Christmas dance.

With her canvas bag slung over her shoulder, Valerie skipped and bounced over to Kristen's house. In spite of the light snowfall before Christmas, it had been the mildest holiday season anyone could remember. That night the temperature still hung around forty-five and the air smelled like spring but Valerie knew better. Colorado weather was deceptive. Tomorrow a foot of snow could fall if a fast-moving storm came in. But who cared what it was like outside? Inside, Valerie felt warm and eager for the evening to begin.

Ringing the McDowells' doorbell, Valerie hid. "Powie!" She jumped out when Kristen poked her head out.

"Valerie! I swear you belong in this family. Noel and Becky have been teasing me for the last hour and now *you* do *that*. If I don't have a heart attack first, I'm spending two days with my sister."

"Changing diapers?" Valerie followed Kristen into the house.

"I've played two different kids' board games three

times each. Diapers will be welcome."

"Happy New Year, Valerie!" Noel jumped down the last three stairs.

"Yeah, same." Becky cartwheeled down the hall.

Valerie dropped her bag and cartwheeled behind Becky. Both of them ended in a heap together, laughing. Before they could get up, Glennie came toward them with a water pistol. "Surrender or drown," she squealed.

Quickly Valerie and Becky scrambled to their feet and ran screaming, following Noel toward the family room and up the back stairs. As they tumbled back down the front stairs, Glennie hot on their trail, Valerie pulled Kristen in front of her for a shield.

"If you get my new sweater wet, Glennie," Kristen threatened, shaking her fist at Glennie, who had pulled up short when she encountered her big sister, "I'll lock you in the upstairs bathroom. And I won't let you out till next spring."

Glennie backed off and went after Noel and Becky again. Kristen turned and pushed Valerie into the kitchen. "Use some of your energy grating cheese, Wonder Woman."

"How can I eat? I wish we could leave for the rink right now." But Valerie went to work with the mozzarella.

"I know you. You can eat," Kristen answered with conviction.

The McDowell dinner hour was like a three-ring circus—lots of bidding for food to be passed and everyone talking at once, the noise level increasing steadily as each family member attempted to be heard.

"Hey, pipe down, gang," Mr. McDowell finally

said. "I like to hear my stomach saying 'thank you' for this great dinner." He held out a slice of pizza, trailing gooey, melted cheese, and bowed to Kristen and Mrs. McDowell. "Besides, we have a VIP guest for dinner. Miss Karate Denver. And if you don't simmer down, I'll have her chop you in half right here before our very eyes."

"Oh, Charles, did you have to say that?" Mrs. McDowell groaned.

"Yeah, lots of blood," said Becky. "And guts," added Noel.

"See what I mean?" Kristen's mother sighed. She was a short, blonde woman who looked a lot like Kristen despite the fact that she wasn't Kristen's real mother. She and her first husband had wanted a large family so badly that they'd grown impatient when for several years after Maggie, the oldest, was born, there were no more children. So they adopted Kristen. The family grew when, two years later, Noel came along.

"Sorry, Valerie." Mrs. McDowell passed Valerie a bowl of salad.

"It's OK. Just so they don't get the idea that karate teaches you to be violent. It's just the opposite. You learn how to defend yourself when you need to, but you also build the confidence not to use the skill except as a last resort. It's even taught me to keep my temper—most of the time."

"Did you ever have a bad temper, Valerie?" Noel asked.

"I confess I did—still do, Noel. But I don't lose it as often as I used to. Some people in this house, naming no names," Valerie said, smiling at Noel and

Becky, "might benefit from it, since it uses up lots of excess energy. All my energy used to drive my mother bonkers."

"And you don't now?" Kristen said under her breath, but loud enough for Valerie to hear. Valerie poked her with her elbow as she raised a second slice of pizza to her mouth.

Mr. McDowell offered to drive the girls to the rink.

"Yeah, we could stop for ice cream on the way back," Becky said. She had as big an appetite as Valerie.

Kristen glanced at Valerie. "Sure," Valerie said. "Why not?"

Yelling thanks, Valerie and Kristen hopped out of the McDowell station wagon at the Ridge Roller Rink. People were streaming in from all directions.

"If my mother had more kids, maybe she wouldn't worry about me so much," Valerie said as they waited in line to get in.

"How come she let you out tonight?" Kristen asked.

" 'Cause she thinks I'm with three girls." Valerie squealed as someone grabbed her and pulled her around. It was Carl, and he kept his arm around her. "You know Kristen, don't you, Carl?" Valerie introduced them again in case he'd forgotten meeting her at Dori's the week before. "I ate dinner at her house."

"Your food budget will never be the same," Carl teased. "This girl can make food disappear in a way magicians would love to learn."

"She burns about five thousand calories a day," Kristen said. "How can you get her to stand still long enough to be in your act is a puzzle to me."

"I noticed that." Carl pulled Valerie even closer and she wiggled loose, embarrassed at the show of affection in public.

"Hi, Carl," Lindsey Lewis called from ahead of them. "Want to cut in up here?"

"Thanks, Babe," he called back. "There isn't going to be room to skate anyway. Want to go someplace else?" he whispered into Valerie's ear. His warm breath on her neck made her shiver.

"Oh, no, I love to skate," Valerie answered. "And all my friends are going to be here."

Carl didn't say anything, but stepped forward to buy Valerie's and Kristen's skating tickets. The girl leaned over the counter to stamp the back of their hands.

Kristen tried to protest, but it was too late. She looked at Valerie, who shrugged. "Look, there's Sunny and Peter. I'll bet they doubled with Dori and Roger." In spite of earlier plans, the girls had not come together, but Sunny had first made sure Kristen wouldn't be going alone.

Sure enough, Roger and Dori spun off the floor to join them.

"What have we got here, quadruplets?" asked Roger, noticing that all four girls had worn white jeans and red sweaters. They didn't usually dress alike, but they'd decided it would be fun for the New Year's party.

Valerie shook her head. She had on earrings that were bells. They jangled loudly enough to be heard over the crowd. "No, just a bunch of dingalings." She laughed and her friends joined in. She wished school would start. She missed being with them every day.

With the floor so crowded, they had more luck skating when the board said, "Couples Only." Carl was a great skater and Valerie loved circling the rink, his arm holding her close, gliding along the floor as one. But he didn't seem comfortable with Peter and Roger and Bill Berger, Peter's friend, so he pulled Valerie away from the laughing, teasing crowd and off by themselves. He didn't have much to say, just stood with his arm around Valerie and watched the crowd.

"Sure we can't get out of here, Val? Go someplace quiet?"

"No place will be quiet on New Year's Eve, Carl," Valerie reminded him. "Besides, I want to be here with my friends for midnight."

"Aren't I your friend too?" He hugged her close and she felt a little self-conscious.

"Yes, but I like the party here." Valerie was determined to stay.

It felt a little like escaping him—he stuck so close— when she went to the ladies room with Kristen. Sunny and Dori were already there. It was almost as crowded as the floor.

"What's with you and Carl, Valerie?" Sunny asked. "Have your own party going on?" Sunny was half teasing, but Valerie felt she had to apologize.

"I think he doesn't like crowds," she explained halfheartedly.

"Maybe he vants you all alone, darlink." Kristen did a bad imitation of a slinky, old-time, foreign movie star.

"Maybe we're leaving him out without realizing it." Dori was always quick to look for a reason for someone's behavior. She was almost too good to be true at times. "Maybe he's a little shy." Dori was an expert on shy people. She had come out of her shell a little since she began dating Roger. Letting people know she was doubling as Bashful the clown when she wasn't just plain Dori.

"You know what Bill said?" Kristen had skated with Bill Berger a lot. "And don't take this personally, Valerie. I'm just reporting. He said, 'Who's the dud Valerie's with?' He said he missed teasing you." Kristen laughed, but Valerie didn't.

Valerie didn't like making excuses for Carl's behavior either, but she didn't like what Bill had said. She especially didn't like suspecting that her three friends agreed.

"Well, he's not a basketball freak. Maybe he *doesn't* feel comfortable with those . . . those jocks!" Suddenly Valerie felt defensive and angry. She swung around and pretended to search in her purse for a lip gloss.

"He's not friendly, Valerie," Sunny said softly. "He doesn't make it easy for anyone to talk to him. We don't know what to say to him. Are you sure—"

"How come everyone keeps asking me if I want to go with Carl? I'm sick of it. Isn't it obvious I want to be with him? Maybe you can't relate to him because you're all such . . . such . . . *children*."

Valerie whirled and clumped out of the restroom, then half stomped, half skated across the planking floor of the risers around the rink. She looked every way for Carl as she skated across one end of the floor against the crowd. She'd left him near the door.

"Looking for someone?" He grabbed her arm.

"Yes! I've changed my mind. Let's get out of here. I can't stand this crowd one minute longer."

"About time," he said, taking her skates as she unlaced and pulled them off. He was gone and back in a jiffy. No one else was checking out. Handing her the bag she'd left behind the counter with her shoes and purse, Carl waited while she slipped on her high-topped sneakers and laced them. Then, taking her arm, he steered her through the crowd hanging around the door.

As soon as they got into his car, Carl pulled Valerie close. She put her anger into their kiss. He misunderstood the reason for her emotions.

"I know someplace we can go." He flicked on the ignition and the engine roared to life.

"I think I'd like to go home," Valerie managed to say over the lump that had formed in her throat.

"You're kidding, Babe! No way are we going home till midnight."

Valerie was torn between getting her way and keeping Carl interested in her. If she really demanded to go home, he would think she was a baby, would wonder why he'd been attracted to her in the first place. But if she went with him wherever he was going, would she still be able to control the situation? While she enjoyed his kisses, that was as far as she wanted to go, and she thought maybe he had something more in mind. As she kept quiet, and they got farther and farther from the rink and Heather Ridge, she was thinking it would be farther and farther to walk if she had to resort to that.

Carl was a sensible person. She'd talk to him, tell him how she felt. That she liked going with him, but that when he wanted to move so fast it scared her. But she wasn't good at talking to people when real problems came up. How often had she stomped out of the room when she was mad at her mother? Had they ever had a real talk about the problems they had?

Landmarks came along that made Valerie realize they were heading for Redrocks Park in the suburb of Morrison. At the center there was a big outdoor amphitheater where stars performed in the summer. She and Kristen, Sunny, and Dori had gone there for a concert once.

Just say no, she told herself as they whizzed along. *Just say no.* Was it that easy? Would Carl accept no for an answer to his unspoken question? Sunny was always advising people in her column to be honest in relationships. Valerie tried to plan something to say to Carl, but her mind just spun round and round till she felt dizzy.

"Whew, I need some fresh air," she said, when Carl pulled to a stop in the parking lot behind the theater. The very dark parking lot. "It's so beautiful up here at night. Let's get out and walk around." She unlatched the car door and hopped out before Carl could say anything or reach for her.

"Hey, Valerie." He caught up with her. "I didn't come up here to walk around."

"I know that, Carl, but it's so pretty. Look at all the city lights below us." She kept walking. "Let's go down into the theater. We might be able to see the whole city."

She heard Carl's sigh as he put his hands in his pockets and followed her. She skipped along as if she came up here every night and loved every minute of it.

"What time is it? Is it almost midnight?"

"Eleven-thirty," Carl said in a sulky voice.

They weren't in the park alone. Valerie had seen another car in the lot. Once she reached the top of the steps that led to rock benches running down and down to the stage, she saw a couple sitting on a bench in the distance.

Finally she sat down. The rock bench was cold beneath her. She ran her hands over the sandstone. Carl sat beside her but kept looking straight ahead. Maybe he didn't know what to do now. He'd probably not dated a girl who acted like this before. Valerie almost giggled. She decided to start a conversation before he got other ideas again. She took a deep breath and hoped she said the right thing.

"Carl, I really like you. I like being with you. The Christmas dance was the most fun I've ever had with a guy." No need to say it was her first real date. "It's just that . . . well, that you're moving too fast for me. To tell the truth, you scare me a little. I'm not like some of the other girls you've been out with."

Carl laughed a little. "No, you're not."

Valerie took a big chance. "You'll have to be patient with me, Carl, or . . . or . . . go out with someone else." There. She said it.

It was quiet for a few minutes. Valerie listened to the slight wind whispering in the huge rocks of the park. She was getting cold. She hadn't dressed for being outside. The rock seat was cold and her jeans were thin.

Carl put his arm around her. She snuggled into the warmth of his body, hoping her actions wouldn't take back the words she'd just said. "I want to go out with you, Valerie. You're so beautiful. All the guys are envious of me. I want you to help with my shows. I'm sorry I scared you."

"It's OK," she whispered, looking up at him.

He took that to mean it was all right to kiss her. It was the magic kiss of the Christmas dance, sweet and soft and tender. Valerie responded, holding Carl closer.

They sat, looking over the city till midnight.

"Happy New Year, Babe," Carl whispered.

"Happy New Year, Carl. Thanks for understanding."

Whether he did or not, he pretended he did. He pulled her to her feet. "I suppose you have to go home now, like Cinderella."

"Yes." Valerie laughed softly. "My mom is really strict."

"I gathered." Carl kept his arm around her as they headed for the car.

He let her out in front of Sunny's house, where lights blazed all over the house, not exactly what it should look like if her mother was home alone. Maybe Carl wouldn't even notice.

She thanked him and hopped out of the car, running up to the walk to Sunny's front door. She didn't know what to do. She'd made a fool of herself with her friends. Then, that surge of emotion had spilled over into her moments with Carl, giving him the wrong idea about her feelings. She really thought she had learned to control her temper, but lately she'd felt more and more out of control.

Valerie felt exhausted, and it wasn't just the late hour. She didn't think she could face anyone else that night. Before someone came out, maybe hearing Carl's car, she dashed off the porch and jogged all the way home even though she knew Sunny was expecting her to join the sleepover. Her mother would wonder what happened, too, and would question her, but with any luck maybe not until tomorrow.

Tomorrow she'd have the energy to handle the other problems in her life. Why did it seem that every way she turned, a new problem jumped up in front of her?

Chapter 12

No one called her the next day to see why she hadn't spent the night at Sunny's. Did no one care? Her mother didn't hear her come in and was gone when Valerie got up.

"Where have you been?" Valerie questioned her mother for a change when she came in around eleven o'clock.

"Oh, Valerie, you're home. I didn't think I'd see you until noon. Ruth and I decided to go out for breakfast. We figured any place in town would be quiet and we were right. Did you eat breakfast at Sunny's?"

"I got breakfast," Valerie answered.

"Did you have fun skating?"

"Sure. There was a huge crowd there." Valerie figured she'd better disappear before the questions got more specific. "I'm going to work out and then shower, Mom. Call me if anyone phones."

Valerie had decorated her room in several shades of green and the colors were soothing. On one dresser sat the trophies she had won at karate tournaments. One whole side of the room was empty of furniture so that she could practice easily. Today she worked out hard for a long time. The total concentration it required took her mind off anything else, and took the edge off her energy. The thought occurred to her that maybe she should take up running too. Right now she felt she could run to school and back without stopping.

"Yaaa." She threw a punch. Then she whirled and stepped, her arms jabbing in the precise movements of the *jion kata* she was working on. *Jion* was long and demanded more strength than any of the *katas* she had learned before.

"Yaaa," she yelled, finishing the exercise. Once her mother had asked her why karate involved so much yelling. She had never watched Valerie practice, of course, nor had she seen a tournament, but she could hear Valerie practicing when she was home.

"Yelling helps focus the energy," Valerie had told her. "And maybe it would scare away an assailant."

Relax, tighten, kick, punch, relax, tighten, kick, punch. Valerie's hair dampened with perspiration. She started to feel better about herself. She was in top physical condition and she liked that.

A long hot shower revived her. She took time combing out her long hair and putting lotion on her skin. A red knit shirt with a scoop neck and tiny buttons down the front suited her mood. She always wore red when she wanted to feel powerful and in control.

But the day was a hundred hours long. Finally she gave up and, without calling first, she walked slowly to Sunny's, taking a chance that she'd be home. On the way over she remembered the vow the girls had taken—to stick together no matter what. Even if they were all dating, they'd make time for each other. Valerie remembered that she had hesitated to swear such allegiance without knowing what demands dating would put on her—how much time she'd want to spend with a guy if she ever met one and he asked her out.

Now she realized she needed her friends, badly. Every way she turned there was a problem to deal with, and she had no one to talk to about them but her friends. She certainly couldn't talk to her mother.

Sunny's brother Davy opened the door. "Haaa-yaaa," he yelled, seeing Valerie. He jumped into a threatening pose.

"Hey, Brat. Looking to get killed?"

"Just try it—go on, try it." He bounced around, clumsily jabbing at her.

Valerie resisted the challenge. "I wouldn't want to hurt you, Brat. Your mom might not like it. Where's Sunny?"

"In her room." Davy let her pass, then grabbed her in a bear hug from behind. "Bet you can't get loose." He held Valerie in a surprisingly tight hold.

"What's going on?" Sunny started down the stairs. "Who was it, Davy? What are you doing to Valerie? Turn her loose."

"She's afraid of me. She can't break loose. I knew she was a ninety-pound weakling, in spite of all her bragging and trophies."

"Explain to this child, Sunny, that to get free I'd have to hurt him. I don't want to do that."

Davy released her reluctantly, still convinced she couldn't free herself. "That's an excuse. You were helpless, admit it."

"I don't need to, Brat. Get lost." Valerie started up the stairs towards Sunny, but she waited till they were in Sunny's room with the door shut to say anything. "I'm sorry about last night, Sunny. Really I am."

"Why didn't you spend the night?" Sunny asked. "We had a great time. Didn't get to sleep until the wee hours. We kept expecting you. You didn't spend all that time with Carl, did you?" Sunny never bothered saying that she accepted Valerie's apology, making Valerie feel less embarrassed about having to make it.

"Of course not." Valerie flopped in a huge yellow-flowered chair filled with yellow and green chintz pillows. "But I did have some trouble with him. I was glad I'd memorized all your columns so I knew what to do." Valerie was suddenly very grateful that Sunny wrote a column in the school newspaper, answering letters from kids with all kinds of problems.

"What *did* the two of you do? Peter's so sweet, I can't imagine."

"I was honest with him. I told him he was scaring me, and I kept talking ninety miles an hour. I don't know whom he's been going out with—he is older and more experienced. I knew I might have some problems because of that, but not so soon."

"Where'd you go when you left the rink?"

"He drove up to Redrocks. I kept thinking it would be a long way to walk home."

"I guess so." Sunny laughed, falling back onto the pillows on her bed. There was an awkward pause. "What—"

"How—" Both girls spoke at once. Valerie laughed, then said, "Oh, Sunny, do you ever feel like every way you turn there's a problem staring you in the face?"

"Of course. Isn't that normal? I'm pretty well out of problems right now, but tomorrow. . . ." She shrugged, hugging her knees up to her chin and making herself into a ball in the center of her bed. "What else is going on besides Carl?"

"My mom, of course. That's an ongoing problem. It's hard to sneak around to date, Sunny. I'll admit that. You guys said it would be, and I don't feel good about it, but what else can I do?"

"You could talk to her about it."

"No way, Sunny. You don't understand—your mom is so neat. It really is impossible to talk to my mother. She thinks of everything terrible that could happen in every situation. Here's the latest . . .

Valerie told Sunny about her father's moving to Boulder. "Right away mom started worrying about my going up there and living with my father. Can you imagine? Someone I haven't seen for ten years, who's hardly acknowledged that I exist. Now why would she start worrying about such a thing?"

"I guess all mothers worry. Your mom talks about it more. She worries out loud. But you're right, worrying about your moving to live with your father is silly. Are you going to see him?"

"I don't know. I guess I might. It's scary."

"Yeah, it would be. Want me to go with you?"

Valerie studied her fingernails, polish chipped at the tips. "You'd do that, Sunny?"

"Sure, Valerie. Any one of us would." Sunny meant Kristen and Dori too. "We're your friends."

"I was afraid I'd spoiled that last night. I've started

to lose my temper lots again. I worked so hard to get control."

"You think we wouldn't be your friends just because you yelled at us? If a person can't yell at friends and family occasionally, what good is it having friends?"

Valerie laughed softly. "Thanks for saying that, Sunny. I need you guys. I've just realized how much."

"We need each other. Hey, this is getting too serious. Let's call Dori and Kristen and go over to Kristen's and play Ping-Pong. I need some exercise."

Valerie jumped up. "Me too. Good idea." She didn't need any more exercise, but she needed to laugh and be silly. Her life *was* getting too serious.

The next two hours turned Valerie's spirits around, and she went home feeling as though she could handle anything that came her way. She continued feeling that way until Monday morning when, at last, school started again.

Valerie missed Kristen since she had to take Glennie to preschool on the way to school. Sometimes she caught up with Sunny or Dori, or they caught up with her, but not today. She rode her skateboard to school alone. Jumping off at the front door of Columbine Middle School, she scooped it up and tucked it under her arm.

Lindsey Lewis grabbed her arm just as she opened the front door and stepped inside. "Hey, Valerie. How come you told Carl you live at Sunny's? He picked me up this morning and commented on how close I lived to you. What's going on, honey? You keeping secrets from him?" She held up one hand. "Oh, don't worry, I didn't tell him the truth. I figured it might come in handy some time." She smiled. "You know we used to go steady, don't you? We agreed to date other people for a while. But I may go back to Carl. Other guys are so childish compared to him. He's really smooth. Know what I mean?" She grinned and walked off before Valerie could say a word.

What was Carl doing, picking up Lindsey, anyway? Valerie felt her temper rise faster than a thermometer in direct sunlight. Valerie didn't know Lindsey and Carl had gone together. Would Lindsey tell Carl that Valerie had lied to him, not in words but actions? Had let him assume she lived at Sunny's?

All day Valerie was so distracted that Kristen asked if she were mad at them again. "No, something came up today," Valerie answered. "I'll tell you later."

Valerie practically ran home after school to get her *gi* for her karate lesson, turning down Sunny's invitation to go to The Speak for their usual snack.

Her mom was home early. "Valerie, oh, Valerie." She started to cry. "Your father called me at work today. He insists on seeing you this weekend. I had to tell him he could take you to lunch on Saturday. Then I couldn't stay at work any longer. It was all I could think about. You don't have to see him, you know. You can call him and say you'd rather not. Or I'll call him if you don't want to."

"I . . . I . . ." Valerie couldn't get the words out. Talk about a day falling apart. Valerie didn't know what to say. Worse, she didn't know what she wanted to do. "I have to go to my class, Mother. We'll talk about it later."

Her mother followed Valerie to her room and

watched while she changed to her *gi,* then put on her down jacket. It was getting super cold outside. Probably a storm coming. Maybe a storm outside would at least relieve the storm inside.

"It'll be all right, Mother. Stop worrying." Valerie watched as her mother stood, wringing her hands, twisting the huge turquoise ring she wore where once she'd worn her wedding ring.

Outside, needing to hurry, Valerie jumped on her skateboard again. Pumping, she flew through the cold air to the bus stop, letting the wind whip through her hair and clear the storm in her head.

Would it be all right to see her father? Who could know for sure? She hurried into the studio, tucked her board, shoes, and coat into her locker, and whipped around. She thought she'd punch the ball or kick the huge tackling dummy that hung from a chain in the hall outside the practice room. But just then Keith stepped in front of her.

"Are you all right, Valerie? You look funny."

Valerie pushed him out of her way. "Of course. Why wouldn't I be all right?" That phrase kept slapping her in the face, echoing round and round in her head. All right. All right.

Pulling back her fist, she punched the ball that bounced between two ropes. Thu-thu-thump. Thu-thu-thump. With rapid-fire fists pounding like machine gun bullets, she struck it over and over.

All right, all right, all right! Everything would be all right. Someday. *About eighty years from now,* she thought. When she was too old to care.

Chapter 13

Keith stopped her again after class. They had sparred silently together, saying nothing, but Valerie worked him hard, kept him fending off her angry punches. She wasn't supposed to bring anger onto the karate floor, but keep it inside while she sparred. She knew that. But what to do with it? She was supposed to focus on precision, or nothing. Better to focus on nothing, clear her mind. But she lost the battle. So much so that Keith dumped her to the floor once when she least expected it.

"Point to McNally," he said and smiled. "Valerie, look, we've been working out together for three years. I like to think we're friends. I consider you to be my friend. Let me be yours. If Carl—"

"This has nothing to do with Carl," Valerie snapped, and was immediately sorry she was being so hard on Keith. He *was* her friend. She was just now realizing it. "We're not supposed to talk while we work," she reminded Keith and went back to work.

"Can I take you home?" he said after class, being persistent. "I have my mom's car. It's really cold."

He gave her a reason in case she protested.

"Yes." Valerie sighed loudly, but with relief. "Yes, take me home, Keith. Thanks."

He said no more, didn't pry into her life again. Just drove up to her front door and let her out. She turned and smiled at him, trying to say it wasn't his fault. "Thanks, Keith. I know you're my friend. Thanks for that too."

"Who brought you home?" Her mother jumped on her the minute Valerie walked in the door.

"A boy from the school, Mother. Give me a break and calm down. Keith is a boy who's been in my class for three years. It's getting colder and I was tired. Is that all right?" Those words again.

"I guess so."

"Look, I'm going to shower. I'm really sweaty, and I'll get sore if I don't have a hot shower. I'll come back down and we can talk. OK?"

"I guess so," her mother said again. She looked awful. Mascara had puddled under her eyes and her hair was messy. An ashtray filled with cigarette butts littered the kitchen table.

"I'm hungry," Valerie said over her shoulder, figuring that fixing dinner would give her mother something to do. She hoped there was something in the house to eat. She *was* hungry. She realized she couldn't remember if she'd eaten lunch or not.

While she showered, Valerie forced herself to make her mind like water—*mizu no kokoro*—one of the basic techniques of karate. She visualized her mind calm like the surface of undisturbed water. The more agitated she'd gotten, the less she could think. She needed to think.

105 🙖

She let the hot water pound her back and neck, took deep breaths, thought of nothing. Then she thought of how distressed her mother was. How did her father feel? Was he only curious to see how this child he'd left behind had turned out?

She certainly was curious. Curious enough to see him? Of course, what harm could it do? And she realized that every time she thought about her father, she became angry. Maybe she could stop that if she saw him. She would be honest, ask him why he left. If he said because he hadn't wanted a wife and a child, she'd then ask why he wanted to see her now.

Pulling on pink sweats and slippers, Valerie realized it was up to her to calm her mother. For some reason—could it be she still thought Valerie might move in with her father—her mom was panicked over all this. She'd ask her mother why she was so scared.

Her mother hadn't made much progress toward dinner. She sat at the table, smoking and drinking a cup of coffee.

"Mom? How about grilled cheese sandwiches?"

"I'm not very hungry."

"Well, I am." Valerie went to work, taking honey-wheat bread slices, spreading butter on one side and placing thick pieces of cheese in the middle. One at a time she slipped the sandwiches into the microwave, watching till the cheese oozed from the inside of the bread. She put the first one in front of her mother without asking if she wanted it. Then while hers melted, she poured a tall glass of cold milk and munched an apple to take the edge off her hunger.

Valerie nibbled her sandwich all around the edges as she had when she was a kid, then popped the final gooey center into her mouth, savoring the tangy, buttery taste.

"You've put too much in your mouth," said her mother.

Valerie laughed inside. Her mother was returning to normal. Her mother had cut her sandwich in half and nibbled one corner. Valerie, knowing that half was probably all she'd eat, reached for the rest. "I'll make you another if you decide you want it," she said in apology for being such a pig.

"I'm fine."

"You're not either, Mom. Why are you so panicked about my seeing my father? You're not still worrying that I might run off and live with him, are you?"

"You won't, will you, Valerie?" Her mother stubbed out another cigarette, grinding it into shreds in the ashtray.

"Mom, I promise you I won't." Valerie decided that, after all, she couldn't handle this attempt at a discussion between them. She got up, gulped down the rest of her milk, and slid her plate into the dishwasher. Then she set her glass on the top shelf and closed the door with a slam.

Maybe her mother didn't even know why she was so panicked. Maybe this was all so sudden that she was reacting to the surprise. She'd get used to the idea in a few days and calm down. Hey, if it distracted her enough. . . . Hadn't Valerie gotten by with riding home from her class with Keith? It wasn't a date but. . . .

A month ago she'd have gotten an hour-long lecture on taking rides with guys. Once on a very cold and snowy day, their neighbor, Mr. McGee, had given her a ride to school. Her mother had found out about it and Valerie had withstood a long lecture on the evils of riding with the male of the species. Valerie's assertion that the McGees had lived next door to them for years didn't seem to matter. Mr. McGee was a male, so Valerie should be cautious.

Fortunately, Valerie hadn't bought into her mother's fear of men. She liked guys, one in particular. She wondered if she could get by with calling Carl from upstairs while her mother was in this withdrawn mood. Would she sit at the table a while longer?

Valerie risked it—and learned that Carl expected her to help with his show on Saturday afternoon. He'd given her a schedule, but to tell the truth, she hadn't had time to look it over carefully.

Quickly she made the decision to have lunch with her father on Saturday, then go with Carl to do the magic show. It would be good to have something to do after the meeting with her father, since she had no idea what mood she'd be in afterwards. She knew, however, that she'd have to reassure her mother she hadn't spent the whole day with her father. It seemed so strange to think about him this much. She'd always handled his absence from her life by not thinking about it.

Should she accept Sunny's offer to go along with her? She debated that for a short time, then realized this was something she had to do alone.

Saturday arrived faster than Valerie wanted. The four friends had gone to The Speak after school on Friday, but Valerie met Carl there and sat with him instead of her friends. She didn't invite Carl to sit with all of them after the experience at the skating rink. Getting the address of the church where Carl was doing his show, she promised to get there early to help set up.

"I'm going to work today, Valerie," her mother said at breakfast. "Will you call me this afternoon, after . . . after . . ."

"Yes, Mom. I'm going to the mall with Kristen and Sunny. They'll mess around while I have lunch. Then I'll probably go home with Kristen. I'll call you from there or wherever we go."

"I don't want you hanging out down at the mall all day."

"We won't, Mom. All of us are broke since Christmas."

"Do you need some money?" Her mother reached for her purse.

"No, I don't need anything." Valerie had told Carl that since he got paid for his shows, he should pay her something. He agreed, so now she would have a supplement to her allowance. She had paid for January's karate lessons with the check her father sent for Christmas. The thrift shops—one of her main wardrobe sources—were usually loaded after Christmas. People cleaned closets in January, preparing for spring.

Valerie promised herself a shopping spree one day next week after school. She hadn't been to the Ritz— one of her favorite places—since Halloween. They had forties and fifties clothes and costumes. She felt the need for something outrageous to counterbalance all the serious stuff going on in her life.

When Sunny and Kristen arrived to pick her up, Valerie was still trying to decide how to dress. "Come on in, guys. I need help." Valerie led them back up-stairs. "Should I dress preppy and conservative, or in my usual way?"

"Do you have anything conservative?" Kristen asked, laughing.

Valerie stuck out her tongue at Kristen. She had a terrible case of the jitters and she appreciated Kristen's trying to make her laugh.

"What impression do you want to make?" questioned Sunny. "Do you want him to like you, or to say, 'Who is this looney? Surely not my daughter.'"

"I'm not sure." Valerie nibbled a nail, already short on account of karate.

Then dress somewhere in between," Sunny advised. "We need Dori. Too bad she and Funky Waganalls have an engagement." Sunny referred to Roger—alias Funky. He and Dori were doing their clown act at the children's hospital all morning.

Thinking ahead to the magic performance, Valerie considered wearing hose and heels, then backed out. If she dressed up too much, her dad might think that fancy clothes were important to her. She packed her costume for the magic show in her bag. Then she pulled on jeans, a blue-and-white striped T-shirt, her jean jacket and, for a bit of flare, a black, big-brimmed felt hat to which she'd added a huge, red silk hibiscus.

"How's this?" Valerie spun around for her friends, then did an exaggerated soft-shoe step.

"You're an original for sure, Val." Kristen grinned.

The girls kept Valerie laughing till it was time for her to leave them. She had arranged to meet her father in a restaurant called Round the Corner, in the mall where they shopped.

"Sure you don't want company?" asked Sunny. "We could hit him up for three lunches."

Valerie shook her head. Her stomach churned so badly she knew she couldn't eat anything anyway. "How would you feel, Kristen, if you had a chance to meet your dad?"

"Scared to pieces," Kristen admitted. "I think anyone would. You know how you tell me you look over your opponent when you're in a karate competition? Figure out his strengths and weaknesses before you spar? Do that to your dad. Let him do the talking. You listen and figure out what he's like, what he wants."

"He must want something," Valerie said.

"Maybe he just wants to meet you, Valerie," Sunny suggested. "Try not to be so suspicious. It'd be normal, I think, for him to be curious about you."

"Yeah." Valerie took a deep breath. "OK, here I go." She gave a thumbs-up signal to her two friends and made her feet walk out of the house toward the mall.

Chapter 14

At first Valerie thought she had arrived before her father. She looked around and didn't see anyone who might qualify—or anyone she wanted to claim. Then from a booth in the corner, a tall, very handsome man rose and came toward her. He had the same dark brown eyes that Valerie had and thick brown hair, styled professionally. He wasn't as tall as Valerie remembered, but then she was tall herself now. Graying slightly at the temples, he was slender and in good shape. Valerie liked that. She was afraid he'd be fat or out of shape. Was he athletic? He looked athletic.

"Valerie?" he said in a soft voice. Was he scared too?

"Yeah." Valerie clutched the lapels of her jacket with each hand to keep them from shaking. She walked ahead of him back to a booth in the corner. Not too many people had gathered for lunch yet, so it was private and quiet.

Taking Kristen's advice, Valerie made her mind *tsuki no kokoro*, like the moon. The moon's light shone on everything, seeing everything. She studied her father, taking in all of his features, his style of dress, his mannerisms. She let no clouds drift in, no anger, no distractions. She calmed her nerves as if this were an important match. It was, she guessed, one of the most important of her life. This man was a part of her. For a time he had influenced her life. She wasn't sure how, but he had been her father for four years.

He'd been studying her too. "You're not anything like your mother," he said finally.

"How do you know?" She didn't know why he'd said that. Had he hoped she wouldn't be like her mother? Did he hate her mother?

"I don't mean that in a bad way, but your mother is pretty nervous, or was when I knew her. You don't seem like a nervous woman."

Valerie liked being called a woman, but she didn't want to be taken in by this man's charm. He appeared to have a lot of charm, a lot of finesse. She didn't even know if she wanted to like him, but she liked her first impression.

"Maybe getting left alone with a small child would make any woman nervous." Valerie threw the first punch.

"Whoa, you're very direct, aren't you?" He smiled.

"It's the truth," Valerie replied, turning to the waitress who appeared before them. She hadn't looked at the menu, but she'd eaten there before. "A guacamole burger with fries and a large cola." She didn't know if she'd feel like eating, but that's what she always ordered.

"I'll have the same." Her dad didn't look at the menu either. "If I eat that, though, I'll have to go run about five miles."

"You're a runner?"

"I ran marathons for awhile. Too old now. Now I go to 10-Ks and more fun races. I got to run in the Boston marathon once when I lived in the East, but I didn't even place near the top. I wasn't in it to win, though. I did it for fun."

"I do. Need to win," Valerie said, still keeping quiet and doing mostly listening.

"You run?" Her dad sipped his water.

"Karate."

"Karate! I thought you were a ballet dancer. You started dancing when you were three. One of my last memories of our time together is of you dressed in a tiny pink dress, all ruffles and frills. You never smiled until your performance was over. I always had to remind you to smile. Are you still that serious?"

Valerie thought about that. Was she still that serious? "About my karate I am. I like it, and I'm good at it."

"Bet your mother had a fit when you switched."

Valerie smiled for the first time. "She did. She still doesn't understand it."

"Does she understand you at all?"

Valerie didn't want to be placed in a position of complaining about her mother, but she didn't want to have to defend her either. "No. I don't think she does."

"I think I'm going to like you, Valerie. You're honest. Thank you for agreeing to see me." Her father played with the paper that had covered his straw. He was nervous. Somehow it helped Valerie to relax, but not to stop throwing punches.

"Why did you want to see me after all these years? Why didn't you want to see me before? Why didn't you write any letters?" The questions poured out.

"You have a right to ask that," her father answered, after a pause. "I'm not sure, Valerie. I guess I was angry when I left."

"Angry at me?"

"Of course not. I was angry at your mother. But I was also angry at myself."

"Why?" Valerie took a sip of her drink. Her mouth felt dry and her throat scratchy.

"I wasn't ready to get married, Valerie. I don't think either of us was. We were pretty young. I was pretty dumb. Your mother kept talking about getting married."

"And you didn't want to?"

"I didn't know what I wanted. Then . . . then she was supposed to be taking care of—of—being careful—not to get pregnant. But she wasn't. She came and told me she was pregnant and we had to get married. She seemed pleased. I didn't know what else to do."

"She trapped you?"

"I'm sure you're old enough to realize it took two." Her father looked at her and smiled, then his face started to get red. "I felt responsible."

"But you didn't want a baby. You didn't want *me*."

"Don't take this personally, Valerie. There wasn't a you. There was only a vague, mysterious something that forced me into a decision. I don't think I knew it made me angry until five years later. Well, I *was* angry, but I wasn't sure why."

"You didn't love my mother?" Valerie challenged.

"I don't know." Her father seemed angry now, but he controlled it. "I didn't know what love was. She was pretty and could be fun when she stopped being cautious, stopped worrying about what might happen. We'd gone together all of our senior year."

"She still worries about what might happen," Valerie said, reaching for the hamburger that the waitress had set before her, thinking about her father's words. She was hungry after all. She licked the spicy guacamole where it oozed out around the edges of the burger.

"I'll bet." Her father reached for his burger too. "Do you two get along?"

Valerie felt like a traitor, wanting to unload her problems with her mother on him. She decided not to go into detail. "Some of the time," she answered flatly, then changed the subject. "You went back to school—to college? What are you doing at the university?"

"I got a degree in German studies. I teach German language and literature. My wife is Austrian. I met her on a bicycle trip in Austria."

"Is she pretty? Mom's still pretty."

"She's tiny and blonde. She laughs a lot."

Valerie realized that her mother didn't laugh much. Had she ever laughed a lot? "Do you have any children?"

"Didn't your mother ever tell you? We have two boys. Joe is nine. He looks a lot like you. Marsh is eight. He has brown eyes and curly blond hair. I dread their being teenagers."

Valerie laughed. She had two half-brothers.

"You're very pretty. I'll bet you have lots of boyfriends."

"Mother doesn't want me to date."

116 ⁊

He nodded. "She's pretty strict? Protective?"

"She worries a lot," Valerie said again. Her father had said that about the boys—that he'd worry about their being teenagers, starting to date. Did all parents worry about their kids dating? All the teachers seemed to worry about sex a lot. That was all they seemed to talk about, yet they wanted the students not to think about it.

As he read her mind, her father said, "It's tough being a parent, Valerie. You may have to forgive us for making some mistakes. There are no advance lessons, and no taking back mistakes we do make."

"Did you make a mistake leaving Mother?" Valerie asked.

"No. But I made a mistake not keeping in touch with you. Not writing to you. Not coming to see you or having you visit us. Heidi suggested it many times, but I thought I wanted to shut the door on my past, forget about it."

"Your wife's name is Heidi?" Valerie smiled. The only Heidi she knew was in the story about the mountain and the goats and Switzerland.

"It really is. I think you'd like her, Valerie. Will you come to Boulder and visit us sometime? Let us get to know you?"

"I—I'll think about it. This is all so strange." For once, she spoke honestly about her feelings with an adult.

"I'm sure it is. I can't take anything back, but I'd like another chance if you'll give me one."

Valerie liked her father—so far. But she needed to think. She wasn't going to make any promises. He might just be super charming, saying all the things he wanted her to hear. She didn't trust him—yet.

"I'm sure you can't even think of me as your father. That's OK. I won't ask you to do that. But maybe you could think of me as a new friend. Get to know me. And Heidi and the boys. Your mother will probably be against it. She said she didn't want me messing up your life as I'd messed up hers. I didn't mess up her life, Valerie. Each of us is responsible for our own lives. We make our own beds, to use a cliché. I don't know what to tell you about your mother's attitude. But maybe you're old enough to make your own decision."

"I make all my own decisions," Valerie said quickly. "I always have. I don't know what I'll do. I . . . I need some time." Just as she didn't let her opponents in a karate match see her weaknesses, see any emotion, she struggled not to let her father see her indecision. She didn't want him to think she cared, that she had any emotion invested in this situation.

"I understand that, Valerie. I'll give you time." He seemed very caring, but Valerie wasn't sure, and she didn't want to get hurt.

"All I've ever had from you is checks." She felt her anger rise, then struggled to push it down.

"I know that too, Valerie. There's nothing I can do about the past. You have a right to be angry."

He always knew what to say. He let her see his emotion. He was saying he was sorry, but what good was sorry after ten years? He had made a new life for himself, one he seemed to enjoy. And now he wanted her to be a part of it.

Did she want to? Could she say, "You're forgiven," and start over with him? She didn't know.

But she knew this first encounter was over. She needed to go away and think about it. She didn't know what she'd do next.

"Think about it, Valerie." He stood, signaling that their first encounter in ten years was over, letting her go. "All I ask is for you to think about it."

"I will." There was no harm in promising that. There was no commitment made. "I promise I'll think about it. Thanks for the lunch."

"You're welcome. You're a strong person, Valerie. Thanks for turning out the way you have."

What could she say to that? Nothing. Valerie turned and forced herself to walk tall and slowly out of the restaurant. She *was* strong. She'd hold onto that.

Chapter 15

"**D**o you know what your problem is, Valerie?" Kristen asked as they headed back home. Valerie had told her friends about her meeting with her father, then called her mother just to say she was OK. "You can't stand agreeing with anyone." Kristen went on, not waiting for a response. "You have to be different. I have a feeling you don't even like Carl Bentson very much, but you keep going with him because your mom says you can't date, and you want to see if you can get by with it."

"I like Carl," Valerie bristled in defense of him.

Kristen ignored her. "Now your father wants to get to know you and you say you're not so sure about that. If I said, 'Do you want to go skating?' you'd say, 'No, I'd rather see a movie.' But if I said, 'Do you want to see a movie?' you'd say, 'No, I'd rather go skating.' "

"Am I like that, Sunny?" Valerie asked, frowning and stomping along toward the bus stop.

"Yep." Sunny grinned. "We said we were getting skates and it took you only two seconds to say, 'I'm not. I'm getting a skateboard.' "

"I *wanted* a skateboard."

"Fine, but be sure you always do what *you* want.
That you aren't being different just for the sake of
being different—or contrary. I read that maturity is
doing what you want to do even when your parents
want you to do it too."

"Oh, you read too much, Sunny Kiefer." Valerie
couldn't believe her friends were talking to her like
this.

On the bus, Valerie dropped her quarters into the
slot and took a seat beside an old man. She wanted
to be alone. Wanted to do some thinking. Besides,
she was getting off two stops ahead of Sunny and
Kristen to go to the church where Carl was doing his
magic show.

"Bye," she turned and waved to Kristen and Sunny
as she got off the bus. She smiled to say she wasn't
mad at them.

"Have fun," Kristen said. "Remember what we
said." Kristen smiled her big smile.

Valerie stuck her tongue out at them and left them
laughing. She laughed, too, stepping lightly as she
headed for the church, once the bus was out of sight.
Suddenly she felt great.

Carl was setting up his table on the little stage in
the church basement. "You're late," he said, sounding
annoyed. "I could use some help."

"Sorry, I was busy. I have to change too." She
hoped that Carl wasn't going to be crabby this
afternoon.

"Go change then. I can finish up here."

In the bathroom Valerie pulled on her navy hose

with the glitter around the ankles and up the outside edge. She slipped into her shiny black leotard, smoothing it over her body, before shrugging on the jacket Dori had made her to wear at the school carnival. She turned in the light so that the glittery material sparkled. The lapels were plain blue velveteen, but the rest was a gorgeous material that shone and sparkled when she moved. The high heels made her feel very grown up. She walked out of the bathroom as if she were eighteen and a cover model for *Vogue* or *Harper's Bazaar*. Tossing her hair back, she approached Carl.

He took one look at her and said, "Looking great, Babe. Here's my extra hat." He tossed her a shiny top hat, and she plunked it on her head.

They pulled the curtain closed not a minute too soon. The first bunch of girl scouts was filing into the church basement, chattering and giggling.

Valerie was all smiles during the show. She bowed, presenting Carl his props with a flourish then whisking them away. She put each one back into the case he carried, which was sitting on a second table. That way, when the show was finished, Carl would be packed up.

The audience of eight- and nine-year-old girls loved him, and it was obvious that he loved the attention they gave him. He bowed to the floor every time the room filled with applause. He winked at the girls and they giggled and cheered. Twice he called for help from the audience and then the girls got shy. He had to be very persuasive. Eventually they would push a friend to the foot of the stage for the trick.

"Great show," one of the leaders said as she came

backstage afterward. She handed Carl a check. "You were very good, Carl. I didn't expect you to be so professional. And your assistant is stunning. Thanks for coming."

"Thank you, Mrs. Frazier. Any time." Carl was gracious. Valerie bowed slightly as she left.

Valerie changed as Carl finished packing up his things, placing his cloak into its plastic bag. "I'll give you a ride home, Val," said Carl, as they left the church.

"Maybe I'll walk," said Valerie. "It's such a nice day."

"Listen, I have a job next Saturday too. Nine in the morning."

"Oh, I have a competition that day, the Denver Open. I can't make it."

"What do you mean, you can't make it?" Carl leaned on the car door he'd opened for Valerie. "You're a part of the show now. You have to come no matter what—the show must go on, you know." At first he was teasing as if he couldn't believe what Valerie had said.

"Carl, this is a big match—the Denver Open. I've been getting ready for it for a long time. No way am I going to miss it, just so I can hand you things. For that matter, you could reschedule your show and come and watch me win." Valerie had taken a firmer stance, hardly knowing it. Both feet were planted solidly on the sidewalk, her bag over her shoulder.

"I can't believe you're going to let me down for some karate meet," Carl said. "You can't be serious about that stuff."

"Why can't I? You're serious about your magic.

Why can't I have something I take seriously?" Valerie was indignant.

"That's fine, but karate? I can't believe you're doing something like that anyway. It's—it's not feminine. It's a silly thing for a girl to do. Next you'll say you want to be a prize fighter."

"Silly?" Valerie tightened both hands into fists. She wouldn't hit Carl, she wouldn't. "Silly? You're the one who's silly, Carl, if you think I'm going to give up anything for you. I don't even like being your assistant when it comes right down to it. It's like playing second fiddle to a conceited actor. And now you're saying what I like to do isn't as important as what you're doing. I should have realized I didn't enjoy helping you when I got so bored practicing. And you know what, Carl?" Valerie whispered when she felt like yelling.

Carl was so shocked by Valerie's outburst that he stood rooted to the spot, but he said, "What?"

All of Valerie's pent-up feelings flowed out like a torrent. "I think I'm already bored with you, that's what. I think I don't even like you. I must have been nuts to think I did. Go find someone who'll stand there and admire you every time you move a muscle, someone who'll be your number one audience. Someone like . . . like Lindsey Lewis! You two *deserve* each other."

Valerie stomped away, leaving Carl staring at her.

"*Now look what your temper has done, Valerie Harding,*" a little voice said.

"*I'm glad!*" she answered back. How could she have been fooling herself for so long? The only problem was that she'd have to admit to Kristen that she'd been right. The only reason she kept going with Carl when she started to see what he was really like was to defy her mother. She couldn't believe she'd done that.

"Hey, Super Woman, want a ride?" a voice said from behind her.

"No," she snapped without turning to see who it was.

"OK, OK. You're walking so fast, you'll get home just as soon anyway. But don't take my head off. What's wrong?"

"Nothing!" Valerie kept walking even though she realized it wasn't Carl behind her, but Keith McNally. He was on his bike, offering her a ride home. How silly. Then a giggle escaped through her outrage.

Keith kept up with her, pedaling slowly. "Valerie, if I could ask you only one question, you know what I'd want to know?" He didn't wait for her answer. "I'd want to know why Carl has been bringing you home to Sunny's, and then you walk home to your house."

"You've been spying on me!" Valerie stopped long enough to put her hands on her hips in surprise and anger.

"I'll swear, I haven't. But I live next door to Sunny, remember? Or didn't you know that? One night I happened to come home at the same time as you and Carl, and naturally I was curious about your strange behavior so—"

"Leave me alone, Keith McNally." Valerie stopped again. "Or I'll punch you out."

"You'll punch me out anyway. You're a fighter, Valerie. I like that in a girl." Keith put out one foot onto the curb and pushed along slowly, still keeping pace with Valerie.

She tilted her chin upward and walked faster. Keith had lost it. Why was he bugging her?

"Roses are red. Violets are blue. My favorite sparring partner is you. Will you be my valentine?"

"No!"

"Will you go out with me?"

"No! My mother won't let me go out with smart alec guys—with any guys!" The truth had slipped out.

Keither laughed. "Ah-ha, the mystery is solved. Well, I'm very good at charming mothers."

"I'll just bet you are. Too bad you're not charming me." Valerie was home at last. She turned up her walk and jabbed her key into the lock. Once inside, she slammed the door.

Her mother was home and came to see what was happening.

"That Keith McNally!" Valerie flew past her mother and into the kitchen. She was starving. "I hate him."

Her mother followed. "You shouldn't say you hate anyone, Valerie. It's not nice."

Valerie stopped in shock. Had she heard her mother say she shouldn't hate Keith? A light went on in her head. She peered in the fridge while she let the idea take hold. Was what Kristen said about her also true of her mother? Were she and her mother more alike than her father had noticed? Was her mother just being as contrary as Valerie all this time? When Valerie had wanted to date, her mother had said no. But now that she'd said she hated Keith. . . . *Hmmmmm*. If

Valerie said she hated boys, never wanted to set eyes on a guy again, would her mother say, "I'm sure you don't mean that?"

Valerie turned and stared at her mother. Why hadn't she noticed the change? Her mother suddenly seemed to be looking great. She was wearing a dress Valerie hadn't seen, and she'd been to the beauty shop and had her hair cut and styled. What was going on?

Chapter 16

"You look great, Mom. Where are you going?" Valerie sat down at the kitchen table with a half-empty pint of ice cream and a spoon. She shoveled in the ice cream as she talked.

"I . . . well, there's a new lawyer at the office. He asked me to go to dinner, and I couldn't see any reason to say no. He'd asked me before and said he was persistent, so I might as well go out with him and get it over with."

Her mother had a date? Was the world going to crash and blow up? Persistent? She thought of Keith and smiled. "Hey, that's great." Valerie licked the chocolate from her spoon and scraped the bottom of the container.

"How . . . how was your meeting with your father?" Her mother lit a cigarette.

How much to tell her? And what to say? There wasn't much. "It was OK. He hopes I'll visit them sometime. He wants to get to know me."

"*Now* he wants to see you. Will you go up there to visit?"

"I might." Valerie decided to use some of the information she'd gained to get her mother to talk to her. "He said you had to get married, Mom. Is that why you're so hard on me? You didn't want me in the first place? I was an accident?"

"Oh, Valerie." Her mother stubbed out her cigarette. "Why did he tell you that? Of course I wanted you." She stared into space for a minute. "The truth is I think I wanted a baby more than I wanted anything. And in those days women weren't so—so daring. They simply didn't have children without being married. Or if they did, everyone thought they were trash. And while you weren't a mistake, forcing your father to marry me probably was. I don't think he ever loved me. In fact, he probably hated me. He wanted to go to college, and when we got married he thought he couldn't. Instead he had to get a job to support me and you and I guess he was right. He did have to. I couldn't work."

"I don't think he hated you." Valerie watched as tears started to roll down her mother's face.

"If I'm hard on you, Valerie, it's just that—that I don't want you to make the same mistakes that I did. And I couldn't bear it if anything happened to you." Her mother got up and stood at the sink, gripping the edge of the countertop, her back to Valerie. Valerie thought she saw her mother's shoulders shaking.

Valerie laid down her spoon and got up, and walked over to her mother. It was fear that was making her mother act the way she did. Valerie could never have guessed that her mother was so afraid.

"Mom, I'm not going to run off with some guy. I've got more sense than that." She hoped she did, but suddenly remembered how she'd sneaked around to go with Carl. "You have to learn to trust me. If I don't go out with any guys now, I might make a mistake later. How can I know what kind of guy I might like to marry when I get out of college if I don't have any experience with them? Had you ever gone out with any guys but Dad?"

"No." Her mother whispered so softly that Valerie barely heard it.

"Did you love him?" Valerie couldn't believe she had the nerve to question her mother like this.

"I thought I did. Yes, I did, and I was so afraid I'd lose him." Her mother sniffed and searched her pockets for a handkerchief.

Valerie handed her a tissue from her jacket pocket. She didn't know what else to say. Maybe it was a good time to tell the truth. "I went out with a guy at Christmastime, Mom. To a dance. I didn't tell you." Now her mother would never trust her. "I thought I liked him a lot, and now I find out I don't like him at all. But if I hadn't gone out with him, I would never have known that. Making some mistakes like that is the only way to learn."

Her mother didn't say anything, just blew her nose and stood there, her back to Valerie. It was as if this were the only way they could talk. Face to face was too scary.

"You can see I'm still here," Valerie went on talking. "I didn't run off with him. I'm safe." Valerie was partly talking to herself. "What happened is that I learned some things that I don't want in a guy. Some things I don't like. He was really selfish and wanted me to do only the things he wanted to do, nothing I wanted to do. I'm not going to see him again."

Had her mother heard her confession? She turned

around as if she hadn't, and said nothing about Carl. She just looked at Valerie.

"Oh, Valerie, I love you so much it scares me." Her mother put her arms around Valerie, making Valerie feel awkward. How long had it been since her mother had touched her?

But Valerie realized something. "I love you too, Mom." She hugged her mother back. "You'd better go fix your face before your new friend gets here. He'll wonder if you were crying because you were sorry you said you'd go out with him." Valerie was more comfortable teasing her mom than talking seriously.

"Oh, my, I wouldn't want him to think that. Can you get your own dinner?" Her mom straightened and smiled, appearing to recover.

"Of course I can. And I have a paper to write by Monday. Maybe I'd better get started on it."

To Valerie's surprise, the next day her mother didn't say anything about her going out with Carl, about her breaking such a cardinal rule about dating. Maybe she was trying to decide what punishment would be suitable. The next couple of nights her mother worked late, so they spoke only in passing. Her mother did ask about school, but appeared not to hear Valerie's answers. Valerie started to get nervous. Was her mom building up for a big blow-up? A new ultimatum about Valerie's life? She wished they could talk again, but Valerie couldn't find an opportunity to start a conversation.

At karate class on Monday, Keith smiled at Valerie but in the warm-ups sparred with a guy who stood next to him. On Wednesday he came in and took a place by Valerie for the stretches, sit-ups, and push-ups. Then he made a point of singling her out for sparring. But both were serious about their karate and worked hard without talking.

"Good work, Keith and Valerie," Al Warrington said to them part way through the class. "Have you two been sparring together outside of class?"

"Oh, no, Mr. Warrington," Keith answered quickly. He grinned at Valerie. "But it's a good idea."

Valerie said nothing. Her mother didn't need to worry. She didn't know if she'd ever go out with another guy.

Valerie went with her friends to The Speak on Tuesday and, under heavy questioning, finally broke down and told them the whole story. No one said, "I told you so." Her friends were as supportive as ever.

As for her mother's mysterious behavior of not yet passing sentence on Valerie's breaking of rules, Sunny said, "Maybe she thinks you learned something already and punishing you isn't necessary."

"That's true, but I wish she'd say it. I keep waiting for an ax to fall on me."

Peter, Roger, and Bill came in after basketball practice and Peter led them to the table where the four girls sat.

Valerie was so quiet that Bill Berger asked her if she were sick. "Sick of your smiling face," she quipped. He laughed and shrugged at Valerie, but sat down beside Kristen. Valerie laughed and was able to join in the banter then.

After karate class on Wednesday, Keith grabbed her arm as she started to race out the door. "Hey,

Valerie, what's your hurry? I'm without wheels and I'm going your way."

"I'm so relieved. I thought I was going to have to walk alone," she said sarcastically, pretending to ignore him as he fell in beside her.

"Listen, Valerie, this isn't a date or anything like that, so stay calm. But I read an article about this guy who competes in karate meets like the one we have on Saturday. He and some of the guys in his *dojo* would dress alike or funny. Once they dressed in white suits and silk T-shirts like big-time crooks. This was before the actual match, of course. They walked into the gym like that. Another time they came dressed like motorcycle hoods."

"Why did they do that?" Valerie was curious.

"It gave them a psychological edge. The other *dojos* would get the impression that they were really confident. It always worked, he said. Well, I thought . . . ." Keith talked faster now. He was excited about his idea. "I—I've seen that you don't dress like all the other girls at school, and I thought maybe you and I could dress up. Like Bonnie and Clyde, for instance. Or maybe you have some other ideas."

"I don't . . . ." Valerie started to say immediately that she didn't want to do such a thing, especially with Keith. Then she stopped. She realized she loved the idea. She did want to do it. It would be great fun. "I mean, I don't know if Mr. Warrington would like it."

"I asked him, just in case. He doesn't care how we dress before the meet, just how we act and perform during it."

"You already asked him?" Valerie was stunned.

"In case you said yes. I thought I'd ask Dick Webber if you said no. I figured we needed some time to plan."

"I'd love to, Keith. But don't get the idea that this means I'd go out with you or anything like that."

"I'd never do that, Valerie. We're friends, though. Right?"

"Sure. Hey, I saw a gray fedora in a thrift shop just before Christmas. If they still have it, this will be an excuse to buy it. I'll wear my charcoal-gray pinstriped suit, and heels." Keith was tall, she could wear heels with him. "And my white blouse with a ruffled jabot." She thought out loud. "I never wore the suit because I thought it was too ordinary, but this will make it different. With the fedora it'll be perfect."

"Ahem." Keith made a big show of clearing his throat. "Maybe I'd better find out what a fedora is."

"A hat, silly. A thirties-style hat. What did you think it was?" She laughed.

"I had no idea. You wear some pretty crazy things, and I didn't want to be laughing for long after we got there. Warrington would kill me for sure. He thinks we'll sweep the awards."

"How do you know what I wear all the time?" Valerie realized suddenly that Keith seemed to know her awfully well.

"I was planning to go to work," her mother said, nibbling a piece of toast.

"Keith McNally is going to give me a ride over." Valerie decided she didn't want to sneak around again, and even though Keith was only a friend like Sunny, Kristen, and Dori, he was a guy. "We're going to

dress like Bonnie and Clyde. It's to worry our opponents, make them think we've really got it together. Keith is a nice guy, Mom, though it may not
have sounded like it when I was raving about him
the other day. We'd had an argument. He's been in
my karate class for three years. He's just a good
friend."

"That's nice." Was her mother listening? Valerie
wasn't sure. She didn't jump all over Valerie for taking a ride with Keith. "Is his dad a lawyer? One of
the lawyers in our firm is named McNally."

"I don't know. If you come to the meet, you can
ask him. I wish you'd come. I might win my division.
You could take a long lunch hour."

Her mother never said she would or wouldn't go
so Valerie left it at that. She knew where Valerie
would be and that Valerie wanted her to come. The
rest was up to her.

Valerie had invited Sunny, Dori, and Kristen too.
They'd been to her meets before, especially when she
thought she might win. Loyal friends that they were,
they always rooted for her.

As she got dressed, Valerie realized she was really
excited. She'd have to work to calm her mind for the
match. But why not enjoy dressing up?

When she heard a car horn, she grabbed her bag
and ran outside. Keith looked great. He wore a dark
blue suit and a gray felt hat. With an eyebrow pencil,
he'd painted a tiny mustache above his upper lip. On
the dashboard was a huge cigar in a cellophane
wrapper.

"What's that on your lip?" Valerie teased, getting
into the car.

"Be quiet, dame, or I'll waste you," Keith growled, frowning.

"I hope you aren't going to smoke that cigar."

"I hope you aren't going to chew that gum and chatter all day."

They kept up the banter all the way to the school. Parking the car in the lot, they got their gear from the back seat. Keith had conned two of his friends who were in the high school orchestra into loaning him their violin cases. He and Valerie had packed their *gis* and other gear into them. They walked into the crowded gym, the cases under their arms like machine guns.

"I see you at The Speak. It's pretty hard not to notice someone like you, Valerie."

Valerie decided not to ask if that was good or bad. Keith's wanting to dress up as a team made her think he wouldn't be embarrassed by her outfits. They really weren't that far out, just not your standard eighth-grade girl's clothes—she hoped. She laughed, remembering Kristen's accusation. She *did* like being different.

Keith took her laughter to mean she was pleased with his idea. "We'll have to go in together. Is your mom bringing you?"

"She never goes to the meets, Keith. She's never seen me do any karate. To tell the truth, she disapproves of it."

"Oh. Well—I could pick you up if she wouldn't think it was a date." He remembered that she wasn't supposed to date.

"She'll probably be working. She works lots of Saturdays. I guess it'll be all right."

"Great. We'll finish ironing out the details after class on Friday. OK?"

"Sure." Valerie felt glad that Keith was her friend. This was going to be fun.

On Saturday her mother did her usual breakfast questioning.

"What are you doing today, Valerie?"

"I have a karate match, Mom. You could come if you like. We're going to be at Heather Ridge High School. It's close. The advanced matches won't start until about eleven. All the little kids will be first."

"Valerie!" screamed Kristen. "That's great."

"Dese friends of yours?" Keith growled with an exaggerated tough-guy accent. "If dere not, I'll waste um for yah."

"Cool it, Clyde." Valerie, acting as Bonnie, snapped her gum. "Dems my best buddies."

"Great hat, Valerie," Dori said. "The Ritz?"

Valerie nodded. "Youse guys gotta cheer loud for us, ya hear?"

"Sure, Bonnie," said Sunny. "And I want you to know we were so afraid of you that we're missing the basketball game to be here today."

"Dat ain't true, Bonnie." Keith poked his violin case into Sunny's side. "Da game's in Cherry Creek. Dis dame is lying."

"We'll handle it later, Clyde. Let's get dis show on da road. I figure we'll moider dis bunch today."

The girls waved and promised to cheer as Bonnie and Clyde went to their respective dressing rooms to change for the match.

Valerie found the section of the gym where her *dojo* would compete and started her stretching exercises

137 ❧

outside the roped-off space. The gym was roped into two rings since this was a big meet and there were so many people taking part.

The bleachers were full of parents and friends watching. Valerie had told her friends where to sit, and she heard them cheer when they saw her. Now she must concentrate, though, focus on her *katas*, her sparring ability. She must make her mind as water.

Her first opponent was a girl she'd faced before. Valerie had beat her that time, but was not overconfident. She took her place, determined to win again.

Bowing to the referee, then her opponent, Valerie took her place behind the taped-off lines. Looking up, she saw her girl smile slightly at her. Valerie did not smile back. She never acted friendly, as if the match were for fun. She never let her opponent see any emotion at all.

Valerie took the first point with a wedge block to her opponent's throat. The second with a triple kick. Then two more for the winning points. The girl had scored none on Valerie. She heard Kristen cheering her, but calmly bowed to the girl and to the referee, leaving the ring with no acknowledgment of anyone else. Kristen knew she had to do this. Valerie would wave at her friends when she was off the floor.

"Good job, Bonnie," Keith whispered to her. "We're winning, easily, and you can win the sparring. I know you can." Keith was never jealous of Valerie's ability. He knew she was better at sparring than he was. He often let her help him with his technique during class.

Valerie did win. She took first place sparring, beating out guys who definitely were not happy losing to a girl. Only then did she let herself show any emotion. When she stepped off the floor after the announcement, she looked around and waved to her friends, then stopped short.

Seated not far from Kristen was her mother, waving and smiling. Valerie waved back. Next to her mother sat an older man, and when her mom turned and said something to him, Valerie knew they were together. Was this her new friend?

"Is that your mom?" Keith asked, knowing what it meant to Valerie to have her mother there.

"Yeah," Valerie said, feeling doubly proud that she had won.

Keith made a big gesture of waving to Mrs. Harding.

"What are you doing?" Valerie whispered.

"I told you I was good with mothers. Besides, that's my mom sitting on the other side of her. Maybe they'll get acquainted. My mother will tell yours that I'm harmless."

"Are you?" Valerie rolled her eyes at her buddy Clyde.

"Of course. Can I escort you to The Speak, Bonnie? Buy you the biggest chocolate sundae they have in honor of your win?"

Valerie stared at Keith for a minute. "Is *this* a date?"

"I'll admit it is." Keith grinned. "Should I ask your mom if it's OK?"

"I dare you to," Valerie said. "If she says yes, though, I'd rather have a double guacamole burger with fries and a large cola."

"You're planning to get fat now that you've won? There are other meets coming, you know."

"I'll risk it." Valerie laughed. And if Keith had the nerve to ask her mother if she could go with him—and if her mother said yes—she'd risk that too.

"What's going on?" Kristen asked as she ran up and hugged Valerie.

Valerie stood watching in amazement as Keith approached her mother.

"You'd never believe it if I told you," Valerie said, laughing.

"After watching you out there, Valerie," Sunny said, "we'll believe you can have anything you put your mind to. You're a good fighter, did you know that?"

Valerie did know that. But she still had some more work to do on it. She still had to get straight which battles to fight and which to settle by negotiation before they got out of hand. As she learned that, she'd win a lot more. ❧

VALERIE AND YOU . . .

by Dr. Steve Bank

This is a story of two Valeries and two mothers.

The first Valerie is convinced that her mother is a hopeless case, and Valerie has stopped talking—and listening—to her. She's sure that her mom is a closed-minded, overprotective bundle of nerves. This is the mother that Valerie has pegged as a flustered fuddy-duddy who never could and never will listen to her daughter. The only way to deal with such a narrow-minded mom, Valerie decides, is to work around her.

But wait a minute! Is it only Valerie's mother who's being narrow-minded here? When we look at Mrs. Harding carefully, we see a woman whose heart is in the right place, even if her way of communicating isn't always positive. Unlike some parents who set no rules for their teenagers, Valerie's mom *has* set some guidelines. And these rules come in handy when Valerie suddenly finds herself in a parked car with a boy she hardly knows. When Valerie explains, "My mom wants me home," she saves herself from a make-out session that could get seriously out of hand.

It's true that Valerie's mother is strict, but on the other hand, she's not impossible either. What we have in this situation are two different people with different views and interests. Though Mrs. Harding doesn't like her daughter's taste in clothes, she doesn't force her to wear preppy outfits and she tactfully says nothing when Valerie insists on dressing like the trendy girl that she is. Nor has her mom forbidden Valerie to go to karate school; she simply doesn't approve of it. And she may be upset that her daughter won't become a ballerina, but she doesn't force her to become one. Valerie and her mom have normal disagreements, but Valerie wins more than she loses.

What seemed like a hard-hearted Mrs. Harding turns out to be a different kind of mom, a woman who wants to hug her child and tell her the truth about the past. This second Mrs. Harding—the softer one—is revealed when a second Valerie takes the risk of communicating her own deepest feelings. Valerie wants to know how her mom felt when she became pregnant with Valerie and whether she had really wanted her baby daughter. And Valerie confronts her dad with some tough questions on where he's been all the years she's been growing up.

By sharing her innermost feelings, Valerie shows she can communicate on an adult level and, in doing so, she earns greater respect and trust. Both shocking and refreshing,

Valerie's honest talk jolts her parents into telling her the truth about their marriage. The second Valerie is no longer a child rebelling for the sake of being different but a young woman who says what's really on her mind.

Do you see a bit of yourself in the rebellious Valerie? If so, you might consider some of these ideas.

- *Arguments with a parent don't have to be all bad.* Disagreements can lead to open discussions and greater understanding of important issues. It's better to try to talk than to sneak around behind your parent's back.

- *Don't mistake how your parent says something with what is being said.* Even though your parent's methods may be a turn-off, you may benefit from some very good advice if you listen with an open mind.

- *Don't be afraid to communicate.* If you, like Valerie, are tangling yourself more and more in a web of lies and deceit, talk things over with someone you respect and trust. And with luck, you will find a Sunny or Dori or Kristen to encourage you to tell your parents what's really going on in your life.

- *Be open about your relationships.* If you like a boy, don't treat him like a lizard, hiding him under a rock so that your parents never see him. Letting your parents meet the boy, talk to him, and get to know him can help quiet their fears.

Valerie's story shows that even the unhappiest situation can lead to growing up. Lies always create unhappiness, tension, confusion, and worry. Like moldy bread that's stashed in a dark drawer, lies only get worse as time goes on. Telling the truth is often extremely difficult but, in the long run, it takes less effort to be open and honest with your family and friends.